The Grand Tour

By the same author

His Lordship's Gardener

The Grand Tour

Ann Barker

ROBERT HALE · LONDON

First published in Great Britain 2000

ISBN 0 7090 6652 X

Robert Hale Limited
Clerkenwell House
Clerkenwell Green
London EC1R 0HT

2 4 6 8 10 9 7 5 3 1

Typeset in North Wales by
Derek Doyle & Associates, Mold, Flintshire.
Printed in Great Britain by
St Edmundsbury Press, Bury St Edmunds, Suffolk.
Bound by WBC Book Manufacturers Limited, Bridgend.

For Mike, Ralph and Sally

Chapter One

'My dear, you seem cold – let us go to your room.'

Flora Chayter looked up at the face of the man in whose arms she was tightly clasped, but the handsome, good-humoured features of Mr Brenner were in shadow, and she could not make out his expression.

It was not the first time that he had made this suggestion. Mr Brenner had been staying at his cousin's house for six weeks, and his flattering pursuit of her had been going on for two-thirds of that time. In public, he had behaved towards Flora with all the formal civility that might have been expected from a member of the family towards the governess of its youngest relative.

During private snatched moments, discreet walks in the garden, and visits to the schoolroom, however, he had soon made his interest plain. This late-night tryst in the garden was only the second such that they had had, and the surreptitious nature of it made Flora uneasy. It was all very well for Malcolm Brenner to say that his cousin, Flora's employer, was frail in health – which was true – and must not be disturbed by talk of marriage and romance until his affairs were in a more organized state. Whatever his reasons, Flora had been brought up to know that no lady should meet a gentleman clandestinely under these circumstances.

The first time they had met in this way – at Malcolm's instigation – had been four nights ago, and on that occasion, too, he had suggested that they go to her room. He had accepted her refusal well; and Flora had thought that the manner of her refusal had indicated clearly that under no circumstances would she permit that kind of intimacy outside marriage. Evidently, Malcolm had not understood.

'Come, sweetheart,' he said caressingly. Flora could well imagine the glow in his sparkling blue eyes, the smile on his well-shaped mouth. 'I'll not hurt you, I promise.'

'I know that, Malcolm,' she replied, not knowing to what he might be referring, but sure that he would not intentionally give her pain.

'Then why not?' he asked her. 'Are we not as good as betrothed? You do love me, don't you?'

'Yes of course, but. . . .'

'But not quite enough, obviously,' he finished sadly.

'No, Malcolm, that isn't true.'

'Then you agree?' he said eagerly.

Flora did not by any means agree, but she seemed to have been manoeuvred closer to agreement without even realizing how it had happened.

'You must give me more time,' she said at last.

'How much?' asked Malcolm, a hint of exasperation in his voice. This whole business had taken far longer than he had expected. Debts and other problems had necessitated his removal from London, and he had taken refuge, as on other occasions, at the house of his cousin's widow. The presence of the pretty governess – a comparatively new arrival – had been an added bonus, but his time here was not unlimited. The chase had intrigued him; but now was the time to bring it to a close. Carefully keeping the annoyance out of his voice, he went on, 'My dear, you must know that it is natural for me to be impatient, just as it is natural for you to have these scruples. . . .'

'Scruples! Well, I'm glad somebody has some.'

A dry, dispassionate voice interrupted them suddenly, and they sprang apart to look, white-faced, at the figure who was even now emerging from the shadows.

'Reluctant though I am to disturb this charmingly romantic scene, I really think that someone has some explaining to do.'

Had either Malcolm or Flora been asked to make a list of those whom they would prefer not to see at this precise moment, then Lord Craythorne would certainly have figured high on either list. As the elder brother of Flora's employer, he was the male authority figure to whom the whole household looked in awe. Flora had only met him twice before, and on those occasions he had been courteous if not cordial, but she knew, as did everyone in the house, that Mrs Brenner would never have been able to maintain her establishment without his money, and Lord Craythorne was not a man to make any kind of investment without taking a personal interest in it.

For Mr Brenner's part, given the choice between Lord Craythorne and Beelzebub, he would have opted for the Prince of Darkness every time, but although Malcolm closed his eyes for a moment, when he opened them, His Lordship was still there, cutting an imposing figure in his riding dress, his whip in his hand.

'Sir!' exclaimed Malcolm, his hand going automatically to his neckcloth, which seemed to have suddenly become strangely tight. 'What . . . what are you doing here?'

'I believe I have already asked that question of you,' said His Lordship. 'But as my reasons are straightforward and, indeed, quite transparent, I will tell you that my sister is expecting me for a short visit. Having been delayed in town, I set out later than expected and have only just arrived. I heard noises and thought I had better come and investigate. I'm surprised you did not hear my approach – but then you appear to have been otherwise occupied.' His tone was still conversational, but strangely enough, this almost made the whole encounter more unnerving.

There was a brief, awkward silence. Flora would have liked to take Malcolm's arm, or his hand, but his arms remained stiffly by his side. She waited for him to say that they were meeting each other because they were in love, but he was silent.

'Cat got your tongue?' said the earl nastily. 'We had better go inside, and then perhaps you can introduce me to your fair companion.'

It was a shock to Flora to realize that he had not recognized her. Of course he could not see her face in the darkness, and if he had only heard Malcolm speak just now, then she could be anyone. A wild idea of flight went through her head, only to be dismissed immediately. Where would she go if she did flee? She would have to return to the house sometime; in any case she could not leave Malcolm to face His formidable Lordship alone. It would be too disloyal.

They entered the house through the door by which Flora had left it a short time before. She had left a candle burning there, ready for their return and, as they went in, the earl, who was taking the lead, picked it up and turned to confront them.

'Miss Chayter!' he exclaimed in astonishment. Then his expression darkened to one of anger mingled with contempt. From the toes of his black polished boots, past his powerful figure in sombre riding dress and his swarthy black-browed face, to his black curls, sometimes tied back in a ribbon, but tonight tumbling past his shoulders in wild profusion, he looked like a dark avenging angel.

'My Lord,' she began.

'Enough,' he snapped. 'We will continue this discussion in the book-room.'

He strode past the kitchens and the serveries, the skirts of his cloak billowing behind him, the flame of the candle in imminent danger as he made very little attempt to shelter it. Malcolm and Flora were hard put to it to keep up with him. Malcolm had neither looked at her nor touched her since His Lordship's arrival. For all the attention he paid to her it was as if he had forgotten that she existed.

They passed through the green baize door which separated the servants' quarters from the family area, the earl standing back with exaggerated politeness to let them through. Once in the hall, Lord Craythorne put the candle down on a table, shrugged off his cloak and, with the ease of one very much at home, threw it on to one of the large Queen Anne chairs and laid his hat on top of it.

'Now, Brenner, a word with you.'

Again, Flora expected Malcolm to say something, even to turn to her, but he was silent. In desperation, she made one final attempt to speak.

'My Lord, I beg of you. . . .'

The reminder of her presence seemed to rekindle the earl's anger. He turned his dark eyes upon her, his thick dark brows snapping together.

'You have been quite busy enough for one night, Madam Governess,' he said. 'Go to your room and remain there until I send for you tomorrow. And kindly have the goodness to refrain from contacting Catherine in any way.'

She touched Malcolm's arm then, but he moved away quickly, walking directly into the book-room. The door closed behind them and, for a moment or two, she stood helplessly looking at it before dragging herself up the stairs.

Once inside the book-room, Craythorne turned to Malcolm and said, 'Perhaps you will now do me the courtesy of explaining yourself.'

Malcolm had now recovered a little from the shock of seeing the earl, and his colour had returned, and with it some of his bravado.

'Upon my soul, I do not think I have any need to explain myself to you,' he blustered.

'Oh upon my soul but you do, sir,' replied the earl, his face like granite, his eyes hard like pieces of jet. 'You have to explain yourself on four counts that I can think of straight away. Firstly, why were you in town when you had given me your word that you would spend time on your estate at Brywood? Secondly, why, despite all your assurances to me, have you got yourself into such a state of debt that your creditors have found themselves obliged to apply to me again? Thirdly, why does your betrothed feel herself so neglected by you that her mother has asked me whether the wedding is still to be or not; and fourthly, why do I now find that you are involving yourself with your cousin's governess? Quite a catalogue of misdemeanours, is it not? Well, sir, where will you begin?'

Malcolm stared at the earl in aggrieved silence. His Lordship was standing by the fireplace, in which the embers of a fire lit to take off the chill of early spring were still burning. One booted foot was on the fender whilst he leaned easily against the mantelpiece. Malcolm always found it galling that although he topped the earl by a good three inches, His Lordship could still reduce him to the nursery with one hard stare. It was this thought that caused him to utter the grievance that was uppermost in his mind.

'Why should you have the right to dictate my actions?' he complained. 'It's devilish unfair that you should have been made my trustee. Why, we aren't even related.'

The earl sighed.

'Most unfair – yes, I've often thought so. Your activities are a vast inconvenience to me. But little though either of us might relish it, your uncle appointed me to act for him in your affairs in the event of his death, and until you reach the age of twenty-five – which mercifully is not far away – I am responsible for your property. But we have had this wearisome debate before on many occasions, and nothing of what you have just said has answered my questions. So let us take the first two together. Why were you in London spending money you don't possess instead of learning about your estate at Brywood, as you promised?'

'I do possess it,' retorted Malcolm hotly, his fair skin flushing as he took a step towards the earl. Some of his blond hair had come out of its confining ribbon and was flopping over his brow. 'Only you will not let me have it.'

'No, and you should thank God I don't, boy,' snapped Craythorne losing some of his patience. 'Thanks to your father's providence, you have a very neat property to inherit, but it is not a bottomless purse into which you can dip, without ever putting anything back.'

'I don't see that you have any right to criticize me,' said Malcolm brashly. 'You spend and gamble. I'd like to know how much you spent on that ladybird I saw you with. . . .'

'You will be silent,' thundered the earl, straightening. He was not tall, but his figure was a powerful one, full of latent strength and also, at this moment, of menace. Malcolm turned quite pale. 'I spend no more than I can afford,' went on the earl in a moderate tone, 'and I think that if you were to visit Craythorne, you would find no land in better heart. I have settled your gaming debts once more – but this must be the last time that I cover for your stupidity. You will go to Brywood first thing in the morning, and learn from Tarrington how to manage it, and if I find you in debt again, and you end up in the Fleet, then I'll wash my hands of you. Do I make myself clear?'

Malcolm shuffled like a naughty schoolboy.

'You wouldn't be acting this way if it were your precious Matthew who needed money,' he muttered resentfully.

'I beg your pardon?' breathed the earl menacingly. Malcolm cast a scared glance at his face, but went on all the same.

'Matthew can have anything he wants as far as you're concerned. You. . . .' His Lordship's cold stare froze the words on his lips.

'Matthew has never, never caused me one-tenth of the trouble that you have, and he works for every penny he gets. You, with a handsome competence and a fine estate, fritter away the good that you have with never a thought for tomorrow. What the devil do you think you are? A butterfly?

'Furthermore,' went on Craythorne a little more mildly after a brief pause, 'why have you been neglecting Miss Ferring? She's a pretty wench, rich, and disposed to be fond of you; indeed, I believe she refused other men in your favour. I thought you liked her.'

'I do like her,' replied Malcolm looking up, 'but it all seemed so . . . so. . . .'

'Well?'

'So settled; so safe; so . . . so dull.'

'Ah.' The earl poured himself a glass of brandy. 'Presumably, your need for excitement would provide the answer to my last question.'

'Sir?'

'About the governess.'

Malcolm looked down, and traced the inlaid pattern on the table nearby with his finger.

'I have one more question for you, and I would like you to think very carefully before you make your answer. Have you made Miss Chayter any promises of any kind?'

Malcolm thought briefly of his assurances that they would be betrothed as soon as he had talked his cousin round.

'No, My Lord, none,' he said.

'Not of any kind?'

'Not at all.'

'So when she met you in the garden, she was simply . . . amusing herself, as were you?'

'That's right, sir,' said Malcolm eagerly. 'None of it meant anything.' He was beginning to relax, but if he thought that Craythorne was finished with him, he was mistaken.

'Very well, then. Let us review the situation. You have frittered away a large sum of money and accrued debts, some of which have been paid from your estate, and some of which have been covered by me personally – no, I don't want your thanks, I just want you to listen. You have caused a deal of annoyance to Tarrington, your bailiff, who had set aside time to spend with you; you have caused distress to your betrothed and her family; and now you have put me to more inconvenience as I shall have to find a replacement for Miss Chayter who will certainly have to be dismissed and so you have also disrupted her life, and that of your cousin and Catherine. You are a very tiresome young man, Brenner, and you appear to lack any kind of sense, or self-control. Well, let us hope that it is not too late for you to learn some. You will leave for Brywood in the morning, as I have already said. I will make your excuses to your aunt, and you will not attempt to communicate with Miss Chayter again. Is that quite clear?'

'Yes, My Lord,' said Malcolm sulkily.

'Then I will bid you goodnight.' Malcolm gave him a resentful look and a stiff bow, then left the room closing the door forcefully behind him. Craythorne sighed, and poured himself another glass of brandy. Not for the first time, he cursed the fact that his strong sense of responsibility would not allow him to wash his hands of one of his most tiresome charges.

Malcolm's father, Stephen Brenner, had been a close friend of the earl, and there had been a spirit of friendly rivalry between Stephen and his brother Claude over the courtship of Maria Barrington. The more flamboyant, spendthrift Claude had won the prize, and Stephen, the reliable, thoughtful brother, had married another lady, who had unfortunately died giving birth to Malcolm. It had always been Stephen's intention that Craythorne should be appointed Malcolm's guardian should the worst come to the worst. But upon the untimely death of his friend, the earl discovered that either through some mischance or because of family influence, Malcolm's uncle had been chosen instead.

Craythorne stood looking down into the embers of the fire, his half-empty glass in his hand, and sighed. Perhaps, knowing Stephen's wishes, he should have fought for at least partial guardianship. But as far as the world was concerned, it was the most natural thing for Malcolm to be cared for by his uncle and aunt. To contest it would have been to cast an unforgivable slur upon his sister and her husband. In addition, he had just taken on the responsibility of two distant relatives, Christine Warren and her ten-year-old son, Matthew. If he were completely honest with himself, he would have to say that he had been somewhat relieved not to have the responsibility for Malcolm as well.

Now, looking at what Malcolm had become, he could not help feeling guilty that he had not had a hand in his upbringing. Claude Brenner had resented the extra charge upon his purse, and never showed the slightest interest in his ward. Consequently, although the boy had been educated as a gentleman, and had received many material advantages, no one had ever tried to encourage in him an attitude of responsibility towards his possessions or those who depended upon him. When Claude Brenner died, Malcolm had just attained his majority, but by the terms of his father's Will, he did not gain control of his fortune until the age of twenty-five.

On his brother-in-law's death, Lord Craythorne, who had been named as an executor, found his affairs to be in an appalling muddle with a number of large debts to be settled. After everything had been thoroughly gone into, there was very little money left, with the result that Maria Brenner's household was supported almost entirely by her brother.

The other responsibility that Craythorne had inherited had been that of administering Malcolm's estate, and giving him his allowance until his twenty-fifth birthday. All attempts that he had made to instil in the young man a proper understanding of estate management and finance had proved to be unavailing. After all, Craythorne was the first person who had ever made such demands upon him. His generous allowance had never sufficed him, and Claude Brenner had handed him sums of money from time to time, to keep him out of the way. Small wonder that Malcolm should resent being made to think about his responsibilities. And yet, how could the boy be blamed, the earl thought to himself for perhaps the hundredth time. The ones at fault were those who had allowed him to grow up in the belief that he could always do as he pleased, and that other people were simply there for him to use as and when he wished.

Matthew Warren, on the other hand, was a very different young man altogether. Under His Lordship's influence from an early age, he had grown up to be a reliable and hard working young man who had hardly caused his guardian a moment's anxiety. Craythorne found it impossible to imagine Matthew creeping off on the sly as Malcolm had done, wasting his substance, and making merry with Catherine's governess. Suddenly overcome with uncontrollable anger, he swore and hurled his brandy glass into the fireplace.

Chapter Two

'I'm very sorry, Maria, but there was no easy way of breaking this news to you,' said Craythorne to his sister the following morning.

Keeping to his usual custom, he had taken an early morning ride, and after a brief breakfast of toast and coffee, he had sought out his sister in her boudoir, in order to break to her the unwelcome news of the previous night's activities.

Mrs Brenner was as dark as her brother, with the same aquiline cast of countenance, but what in him was swarthiness was manifested in her as an unhealthy sallow complexion. She was as languid as he was vigorous, and as indecisive as he was determined.

A difficult delivery of Catherine, her only child, twelve years before, had resulted in her taking to her bed, and as she and her husband had never had anything in common, she had never received any encouragement to get out of it. She was now so used to being an invalid that she would have found it rather strange to be anything else.

She looked quite shocked at the news, but merely said, 'Leigh, are you quite sure? Perhaps a mistake. . . .'

'Absolutely sure, unless you would have me doubt the evidence of my own eyes.' He strode back from the window to the bed. 'I caught them myself.'

'Poor Malcolm,' murmured Mrs Brenner.

'Malcolm?' repeated her brother incredulously. 'I would have thought that Miss Chayter was more deserving of pity.'

'That designing hussy,' she replied. 'I might have guessed that she would get her claws into him. And I had hoped that she would stay with us until Catherine's come-out.'

Maria Brenner was a past master at avoiding worry and distress, usually by shuffling her problems onto other people's shoulders. Now she said in a tired voice, 'I suppose she will have to go, but dealing with such matters is so wearing. Leigh, I do not suppose that you. . . ?'

Craythorne smiled wryly.

'I'll dismiss her if you want me to; after all, I've already sent Malcolm packing,' he said, in the tones of one to whose lot it generally fell to deal with matters which his sister found unpleasant. 'The only thing I would like to know is how this affair has been allowed to progress to such an advanced stage apparently under your very nose.'

Mrs Brenner leaned back against the pillows and looked suddenly breathless and exhausted.

'Leigh, my dear, you know how ill I am, and especially in spring.' (Here, the earl nobly repressed the thought that whatever the time of year, Maria would have found it particularly injurious to her health.) 'It has been as much as I have been able to do to get up for dinner whilst Malcolm has been here – and even then, I have not always managed that.'

The earl looked incredulous.

'You mean that that young wastrel has been allowed to run tame in this house, with no one to check what he was doing?'

'I thought that you would be pleased he was not in London,' replied his sister defensively, as she reached for her vinaigrette. 'I know how concerned you have been about his gaming. And he is company for Catherine. . . .' Her voice tailed off.

'Not just for Catherine, evidently,' said Craythorne drily.

Seeing that she was making herself look more neglectful of her duty than ever, Mrs Brenner fell back on her last weapon.

'Leigh, please go away,' she murmured, leaning back against her pillows as if she were at her last gasp. 'You have so much energy that you almost wear me out.'

'Very well, my dear,' answered Craythorne, seeing at once that the audience was now concluded. 'And don't worry; I'll go and do the deed for you.'

As he left his sister's room, however, he was conscious of a certain reluctance to send for the governess. Among society in general, he was held to be a hard, rather cold man, but those who served him knew him to be just and scrupulously fair. It was not that he did not feel that Miss Chayter should be dismissed; she had demonstrably behaved in a way that was not acceptable for a respectable young woman in her position. For all he knew, she might even have been neglecting Catherine in order to pursue her amours. His chief concern was that his acquaintance with Miss Chayter was not of very long standing, and what he had seen he had liked, whereas he did know Malcolm Brenner very well, and what he knew made him very distrustful of the young man's motives, despite the protestations that he had made the previous evening.

In his abstraction, he found that he had made his way to the schoolroom, and he wandered in to find Catherine reading. She was not a pretty child, but her complexion was clear and her long dark hair was straight and shining, and Craythorne realized for the first time that she might grow up to be a very handsome woman.

'Hallo, Catherine,' said the earl.

'Oh, hallo, Craythorne,' said the child, getting up dutifully to curtsy, then to offer him a kiss. The earl disliked being called 'uncle' and had encouraged Catherine from an early age to address him by his title, as did his contemporaries.

'What are you reading?' asked the earl, picking up her book.

'Just a little of the *Aenead*,' she replied matter-of-factly. 'Only I am a little stuck here, until Miss Chayter comes to explain it to me.'

'Let me see if I can help,' he replied. His Latin was a little rusty, but he was just able to provide the required assistance.

'Do you go to the vicar to learn Latin?' he asked her.

'Oh no,' replied Catherine, laying down her book and sitting opposite him. 'Miss Chayter teaches me everything. We have been studying French and Italian and Miss Chayter thought that if I learned Latin, it would help me understand more about the roots of language. You see, many of the words that we use every day have Latin sources.'

'Really,' murmured the earl, looking round the little schoolroom as she spoke. Everywhere there was evidence of scholarship and order, from the neat row of well-kept books, to the globe in the corner and the sketches on display.

'Yes,' said Catherine. 'I wanted to learn Greek as well, but Miss Chayter says that I ought to wait for a little while.'

'She is probably right,' said the earl. 'Tell me, what do you enjoy most about your lessons with Miss Chayter?'

'We have been making a Grand Tour,' confided Catherine.

'Indeed?' queried the earl, looking puzzled. He had not heard that Catherine and her governess had travelled anywhere together.

'You see, a lot of young men when they reach the age of about seventeen travel abroad for their education,' explained Catherine. The earl, who had made such a journey some twenty years before, listened courteously. 'Girls don't do so, but Miss Chayter said that if we pretended to go on such a journey, we could learn a lot. When we were travelling through France, we spoke a lot in French and I have been looking at some of the books in the library and making sketches.' She crossed the room to fetch her sketchbook and brought it back for the earl to see. The picture of Notre Dame was quite well executed, if a little wobbly.

'And are you still in France now?' asked the earl, as he looked at some of the other drawings.

'No, we have just journeyed into Italy,' she replied. 'So now we are conversing in Italian, and we have been reading about some of the travel experiences of ancient writers. Miss Chayter makes it all such fun. Only. . . .'

'Yes?' prompted Craythorne, wondering if he was about to hear of some neglect taking place whilst Malcolm had been here.

'I am so afraid that she will go away,' said Catherine all in a rush. 'I heard two of the maids talking and saying that she might have to do so.'

Marvelling at the speed at which news could travel, especially if it was something scandalous, he said carefully, 'Did they say why?'

'No,' she answered. 'I do hope she doesn't. We haven't nearly finished our tour yet, and she makes it all so interesting, and she knows about all kinds of things. Some of my other governesses. . . .'

'Well?' prompted the earl.

'I think I knew more than they did,' confessed Catherine.

Reflecting with a sigh of resignation that no doubt the news that her beloved governess had left would have to be broken to Catherine by him, he made his excuses, and went down to the book-room to prepare for an unpleasant interview.

Descending the stairs, Flora Chayter looked neat and composed, if rather pale. She had not slept well that night for her mind had been filled with speculation as to what had been said behind that closed door after she had gone upstairs. She had waited up for a long time, half expecting Malcolm to come and tell her what had happened, but he had not appeared. She thought anxiously about how intimidated he must have felt in face of His Lordship's wrath. She knew instinctively that Malcolm was not a strong person, and that when they married, she would have to be strong for him. She sighed a little, wishing that he could have found the courage to speak up for them both last night, and that perhaps he might have insisted that they go in and confront the earl together; then she would not have had that ghastly, sleepless night to go through. However, that had not happened, and it was no use repining. At least it would be all out in the open now. Perhaps Malcolm would be waiting for her outside the book-room, ready to go in with her, or maybe he would be in there already.

For a brief, heady moment, she imagined the earl's rather thick lips curved upwards in a benevolent smile as he gave them his blessing. Then she smiled herself, but ironically, without humour. He would be far more likely to show them both the door. Well, they would manage – she would see that they did. She squared her shoulders.

Malcolm was not waiting outside, so she gathered all her courage together and knocked on the book-room door. On hearing Craythorne's voice, she opened it and walked in. The earl was the room's only occupant. He was sitting at the desk near the window perusing a document. He did not rise, but nodded in response to her curtsy and said, 'You may be seated, Miss Chayter.'

After she had been sitting for what appeared to be an eternity, but was probably less than a minute, he put down the document, got up, walked round to the other side of the desk, and perched on the corner of it, his arms folded. He was not a handsome man – indeed, some termed him downright ugly – but there was something impressive about his broad-shouldered, powerful figure, and there was an air of suppressed energy about him that could often be compelling, and at times – as now – quite intimidating.

'I am seeing you on behalf of my sister and at her request,' he said. 'Believe me, Miss Chayter, when I tell you that she is quite appalled at your conduct and very disappointed in you, and I have to say that my sentiments are the same.'

Flora blushed.

'I am very sorry, My Lord,' she said, looking down at her hands, and wishing very hard that Malcolm would arrive soon. 'We were very wrong. . . .'

'You were indeed,' replied the earl with a hint of a sneer. 'Clandestine meetings are to be expected in a very young, foolish girl – but you have neither of those things to excuse you. You do not even have the excuse of having been led astray.' He paused for a moment as if expecting her to say something, then when she was silent, he went on, 'You have been placed in this household in a position of trust and you have betrayed that trust.'

Flora still sat looking at her hands. Where was he? she wondered. Why did he not come? Almost involuntarily, she said his name.

'Malcolm. . . .'

'Ah yes,' said His Lordship. 'That, I think, is the part that angers me the most of all. Because in you, quite frankly Miss Chayter, we appeared to have found a governess who was satisfactory in every way, and you have intrigued yourself with, I regret to say, one of the most worthless young men with whom it has been my misfortune to deal. To be honest, I was not at all sorry to send young Brenner packing, but—'

He broke off as Flora rose to her feet, turning white.

'You have . . . sent him away? He has gone?'

'Certainly he has gone,' returned Craythorne, his sneer even more pronounced. 'You cannot suppose that I would permit further opportunities for love-making beneath my sister's roof?'

Miss Chayter had missed supper the previous night because she had not felt well. That morning, the thought of the coming interview had effectively removed her normally healthy appetite. Consequently, the shock of hearing that Malcolm had gone, coupled with the effect of her standing quickly made her suddenly feel faint. It was as well that the earl was standing close by, for he caught her as she fell and carried her to a leather couch where, after a sip or two of brandy, brought to her by the earl, she began to recover her composure.

She opened her eyes to discover Lord Craythorne scowling down at her with a serious but not unkindly expression on his face.

'Have you eaten this morning?' he asked her abruptly. She shook her head. 'Then you will do so immediately. I've no desire to have your death on my conscience. Come, take my arm.'

Flora did as she was bid, conscious as she did so of the hard strength of his frame. He escorted her to the breakfast parlour, from whence the servants had long since cleared away the remains of the meal. Looking round impatiently, the earl grunted, then rang the bell.

'What do you require for breakfast?' he asked her, surprising her so much that she nearly jumped out of her skin. She had not expected her wishes to be considered at all today.

'Some . . . some coffee and bread and butter, if you please,' she answered.

He gave the order as requested to the servant who came, then added, 'I have letters to write so will leave you now. Please return to the book-room when you have finished – and for goodness sake, eat that food I've ordered. I don't want you fainting again.'

On his return to the book-room, Craythorne did sit down at the desk, and took a sheet of paper ready to write, but instead, he sat gazing into space. The girl had certainly been shocked at Brenner's departure. She had almost fainted, and had even looked nauseous for a time. Could Brenner have left her with child? Having discovered the length of Malcolm's stay, the earl did a little mental arithmetic. Perhaps not enough time had elapsed for her to feel such symptoms, but nevertheless, the possibility was there. It would be typical of the puppy to have done so, he thought to himself savagely.

In any case, his course of action was quite clear: he should throw her out immediately without wages or references, and give her plight no further thought. Scarcely a soul among his friends and acquaintances would blame him for such a deed. The problem lay, not with the judgements of his contemporaries, but with the dictates of his own conscience. There was more than a hint of the philanthropist about Lord Craythorne, and some of the projects that he supported would have very much surprised some of those in his social circle.

Angrily he thumped the desk in front of him, and swore. He had no patience with puppies like Malcolm Brenner who played games with other people's lives, and escaped the worst consequences, shufling them instead onto other people, apparently without a second thought. Yes, he did have it in his power to make life very difficult for Malcolm, but the problems that young Brenner would face would be as nothing to the difficulty Flora Chayter would experience in finding other employment, possibly with a baby on the way.

There was another problem that concerned him, and that was finding another governess for Catherine – a task which would inevitably fall upon his shoulders. Two years ago, Catherine had been withdrawn and obstinate, and her governess had written her off as being backward. Taking the advice of a childhood friend, Mrs Letitia Wylde, he had employed Flora Chayter. Now, Catherine was revealed to be bright, friendly and communicative.

'Damn Brenner,' declared the earl, thumping the table again. Now the search for a governess for Catherine would begin all over again, Maria would no doubt have hysterics, and everything would fall upon his shoulders as always. His only hope was that it would be sorted out in the next few weeks, because very soon he would be unavailable to help.

In the breakfast parlour, Flora consumed her meal as quickly as possible. She had not thought that she would be able to eat, but once the food had arrived, she realized how very hungry she was. Although the servants were as courteously impassive as ever, Flora thought that she detected beneath their impassivity a thinly veiled contempt. She almost felt that she would be glad to return to the company of Lord Craythorne. There, at least, the distaste that he felt for her actions was clearly on view. She was also confused about Malcolm's leaving without her. She would have to wait until the earl explained to her more clearly what had happened.

On her return to the book-room, she paused briefly before knocking, reflecting that this was becoming something of a habit. Inside, Craythorne was now standing by the window, his expression impossible to read against the light. He had the advantage therefore of being able to study her. She was of medium height for a woman, small-boned but healthy-looking, with ash-blonde hair, which persisted in escaping from its confinement, however severely she sought to control it. Her face was heart-shaped, and her features were regular. Looking at her, the earl had no difficulty in understanding why Malcolm wanted to intrigue himself with her, but he told himself severely that that was beside the point.

'Have you now broken your fast?' he asked her. She nodded. He gestured for her to be seated once more. 'I gather from your reaction earlier that you did not expect Brenner to have gone.'

'I am not surprised that you sent him away,' she said in a low voice, her head bowed. 'Nor do I expect to be treated any differently after the way I have betrayed your trust, but I had hoped that you might have allowed us to leave together.'

'To set up house, no doubt,' returned the earl contemptuously. 'I expect he neglected to inform you that he does not have a feather to fly with!'

Flora looked up then, her face flushing.

'He did inform me of it,' she replied. 'I know that he is not a wealthy man, My Lord.'

'He would be wealthy enough if only he would be more prudent,' murmured Craythorne, as he walked round to the other side of the desk. 'He told me that you were both amusing yourselves in this relationship. Obviously your idea of amusement differs somewhat from any other lightskirt of my acquaintance. Tell me then, Miss Oh-so-prim-and-proper-Chayter, how did you suppose that he would manage to support you as his mistress and provide for a wife as well?'

'A wife?' Flora's hand went to her throat. Her blonde, fluffy hair was escaping from its severe confinement, her hazel eyes wide with shock, her face whiter than ever. Her air of vulnerability somehow kept Craythorne's anger hot, although he would have found it impossible to say why.

'Did he omit to mention the fact that he is betrothed?' he asked her savagely. 'Don't tell me that you really believed that a man like Brenner with such expensive habits would seriously look twice at a penniless governess! Obviously, Brenner lied when he told me that you were both amusing yourselves. He was having the fun – and you were being played for a fool. Anyone with more than an acorn cup of common sense would have realized that straight away.'

'Then clearly, I am uncommonly foolish,' Flora replied, pleased in an oddly detached sort of way that her voice did not wobble.

There was silence in the room for a short time. The earl looked once more at Flora Chayter as she sat with downbent head, her whole posture one of dejection. She was just a young woman, little more than a girl really, dressed discreetly if unbecomingly, in a gown of gun-metal grey. Damn Brenner, Craythorne thought to himself again. He sighed audibly.

'I am not a fool, Miss Chayter,' he said in much calmer tones. 'I am fully aware of the fact that Malcolm is just as guilty as you are, but the fact remains that I cannot tolerate scandal or scandalous behaviour to touch this house, and more particularly to affect my niece, and for this reason I cannot do other than dismiss you.'

Flora's heart sank. She had not really expected anything else, but for all that, it was still a blow.

'If it is any consolation to you,' he went on in his harsh voice, 'Mr Brenner will not go unpunished.' She looked up at him. There was a directness in her gaze that he would ordinarily have found very appealing.

'It would be a very strange person who found comfort in the punishment of others,' she said quietly.

'On the contrary, it would be a very normal person,' he retorted. 'Unless of course you still imagine yourself to be in love with him.'

Flora did not reply. In truth, her feelings about Malcolm Brenner were now so confused that she would have been hard put to it to voice them.

'There is just one more thing that I need to know from you,' said Craythorne, returning to the window and standing with his back to her. 'I would like you to tell me if you think that there is any chance of your being with child by Mr Brenner.'

Flora stood up, her face flushed this time with indignation.

'My Lord, you are entitled to dismiss me, but I cannot accept that you are entitled to enquire into my concerns any further.'

The earl turned to look at her.

'You do not deny it, then,' he said.

'I have no intention of saying any more on the subject.'

'Very well then,' returned the earl after a tiny pause. 'Far be it from me to invade your privacy. As you say, it isn't really any of my business. If it should turn out to be the case, however, you had best come to me rather than to Malcolm. He never has any money, and if he did have any, I doubt he'd give it to you. You had better go and pack your things. I will calculate what sum of money is owing to you and make sure that you receive it before you go. Leave your address, and your trunk will be sent on to you.'

She looked at him with an expression of surprise on her face. He came away from the window and she saw that he was smiling grimly.

'I have told you that I am not a fool, Miss Chayter; I have no wish to hear of your dying in a ditch on my account.'

There appeared to be no more to say. Flora curtsied to him for the last time.

'I am so very sorry, My Lord,' she said.

'So am I, Miss Chayter,' he replied.

Chapter Three

'Dismissed! Flora, my dear! But why?'

Until now, Flora had managed to retain the rigid self-control that had sustained her from the moment of her departure from the book-room. She had not been allowed to say good-bye to Catherine – which was perhaps a blessing, as it would have been painful for them both, and Flora would not have had any idea what she might say to her. No one had seen her off. The footman had handed her a packet addressed to her in Lord Craythorne's careless scrawl. He had done so with a slight curl of the lip which might have indicated insolence.

She had left the house with only one small bag – the rest of her property was to follow later. Luckily one of the grooms was going to Canterbury that day for supplies, so she was able to ride with him and catch the stage which had taken her to Bishops Bourn. The journey was mercifully short, being only one stage, and from there she had been able to walk the short distance to Biddlecombe Rectory, the place that had been home to her ever since her parents had died. She was greeted by Mrs Wylde with surprise and pleasure.

'Flora, how lovely! And just as I was thinking about dear Jane and wishing that I could be with her, especially with the first baby on the way! But how comes this about? Have you been given a few days' holiday?'

Flora straightened her shoulders.

'No, I'm afraid not, ma'am,' she said evenly. 'I have been dismissed.'

It was Mrs Wylde's horrified exclamation that caused Flora's composure to crumble, and at once she burst into tears. Immediately, Mrs Wylde was bustling about, undoing her bonnet strings and taking off her cloak.

'My dear, pray don't distress yourself! Come and sit down and have a cup of tea. When did you set off?'

'This morning,' managed Flora between sobs.

'Then you must be hungry. I will ring for tea and bread and butter and then you will feel a little better and will be able to tell me all about it.'

Whilst Mrs Wylde was giving the orders for tea and passing Flora's outdoor things over to be taken to her room, Flora got up and went to look out of the window, anxious that none of the servants should see her tears and perhaps guess their cause.

Outside in the garden she could see the summer-house where she and Jane had played at tea-parties years ago. Flora's parents had died when she was six, and Mrs Wylde, having been at school with Flora's mother, had taken the child in and brought her up as her own. Jane, the Wyldes' only daughter was the same age, within a few weeks, and could easily have been jealous, and made Flora feel unwelcome. Instead, with all the generosity that comes from a naturally sunny nature, she had treated the newcomer like a sister from the very beginning. What happy times they had spent together, she and Jane!

Nevertheless, Flora reflected, all this could not alter the fact that Mrs Wylde was not related to her in any way. For all her warm nature, Mrs Wylde was a woman of high principles. She might easily be as horrified at her behaviour as Lord Craythorne and show her the door. Flora could not delude herself: parents had been known to turn their own children out of doors for such a cause. Within a very short time, she might find herself a stranger to the only home that she could remember.

The closing of the door signalled the departure of the servant, and soon she heard Mrs Wylde's voice saying, 'Come along now, tell me the whole story.'

Flora went obediently and sat down next to her on the sofa. She told her benefactress everything, trying to be completely honest, even including the stolen kisses she had shared with Mr Brenner and Lord Craythorne's insulting questions. When her account was over, her listener sat in silence for a few minutes, then said, 'Flora my dear, there is no doubt at all that you have been very foolish, is there?' Flora shook her head, feeling tears starting to her eyes at the gentleness of the older lady's tones.

'I am very well aware that I have behaved very badly,' she admitted, as she fumbled with the strings of her reticule and took out her handkerchief.

'Foolish was the word I used, and I stick by that,' replied Mrs Wylde firmly. 'But you were not the only foolish one in the business. What was Maria Brenner about to allow such a state of affairs to come to pass?'

For a moment, Flora was startled to hear Mrs Wylde refer to her former employer by her Christian name, until she recalled that in her girlhood when she was still Letitia Gooding, she had lived near to the Craythorne estate and had played with the young Maria Barrington, as she had been then, and her formidable brother.

'She does not enjoy good health,' began Flora. Mrs Wylde gave a snort.

'No, she enjoys bad health – and enjoy is exactly the right word! She has been fancying herself ill for years. Even as a girl, she had that droopy, die-away air and I might have guessed how she would turn out, if I had not been so busy climbing trees with Leigh! If she would only bestir herself and take the reins of the household into her hands rather than leave every day-to-day thing to the servants, and rely on Leigh to take the important decisions, then she might have more to think about than the state of her health.'

'Was Mrs Brenner always rather languid?' enquired Flora, momentarily diverted from her unfortunate situation.

'Oh yes, always. Her mother thought it ladylike and encouraged it, whereas Leigh – Lord Craythorne as he is now – was encouraged to come to the vicarage and run tame with my brothers, and I did have four of them!'

'What was Lord Craythorne like as a playmate?' asked Flora curiously. She found it difficult to imagine the nobleman who had dismissed her as a grubby schoolboy.

'Rather more tolerant of me than my own brothers,' confessed Mrs Wylde. 'It was not Leigh who put a frog down my back, after all! But they were all very good, and never made me feel excluded just because I was girl.' She was silent for a moment, lost in reminiscence, then she pulled herself together. 'But that is not at all to the purpose. The point is that you, an innocent young girl, were left unprotected, open to the advances of a practised seducer.'

'Oh no!' exclaimed Flora.

'Oh yes,' contradicted her companion firmly. 'I may not be at the hub of the social scene here, but I keep my finger on the pulse of things, let me tell you, and I have heard a few things about young Malcolm Brenner, and none of them to his advantage. A practised seducer with no interest in anything except his own satisfaction.' She became aware that Flora was sitting with her head bowed, and she went on more gently, 'Perhaps I should not have been so blunt, for I cannot suppose that you would have allowed him to take such liberties if you had not thought yourself to be in love with him.'

Flora looked up then, her eyes filling once more.

'I believed it to be so,' she admitted. 'But then I also believed that he loved me in return. The news of his departure was such a shock to me that I fainted when Lord Craythorne told me of it.'

'You fainted? How came you to do such a thing? I have never known you to do so before.'

'I had fasted since the previous day,' admitted Flora. 'I stood up too suddenly, I think.'

'I trust you did not hurt yourself when you fell,' said Mrs Wylde concernedly.

'No, for Lord Craythorne caught me,' replied Flora flushing.

'That must have been a shock for him,' put in Mrs Wylde with a chuckle.

'He was very practical in dealing with the situation,' acknowledged Flora. 'He gave me some brandy, then made sure that I was served with something to eat.' She thought for a few moments then went on, 'I do not blame him for dismissing me. What else could he do?'

'Quite a few things I should say – beginning with putting the blame fairly and squarely where it belongs – on the shoulders of young Brenner. But tell me, Flora, how do you feel about him now?'

Flora considered the matter carefully. 'I cannot change my feelings so quickly as he appeared to do,' she admitted. I still feel some . . . tenderness towards him. I could not help being attracted to him. He is so handsome and charming, and he seemed to be genuinely interested in me; and perhaps he was, despite his betrothal. But I cannot forget the fact that when it came to the point when Lord Craythorne confronted us, he could not stand up to him or support me.'

'Of course, Leigh is a formidable man,' put in Mrs Wylde.

'Yes, I know, but a man who was truly in love would have braved his anger.' There was a short silence, then she went on in a rush, 'Aunt Letty, you can't think how pleasant it was to have another person of my own age to talk to! Catherine is a lovely girl and I will miss her terribly, but there were ten years between us in age and besides she is – was – my pupil. To have someone who could be a friend – to laugh with. . . .' Her voice tailed off.

'You still miss Jane, don't you?' said Mrs Wylde quietly. Flora nodded. After a brief silence, Mrs Wylde went on in a more energetic tone, 'Well now, we must bestir ourselves. I shall tell the housekeeper that you are here on a long stay because of family matters that your employer wishes to sort out. That's true – after a fashion, and it will take care of servants' gossip. The same story more-or-less will do for Peter. He would not understand the predicament you were in. Men,' she went on sweepingly, 'have very little understanding of such matters. For the long term, we will have to put our thinking caps on, for you may recall from my letters that I am due to pay a visit to Jane in Venice very soon.'

The next few minutes were spent in discussing this agreeable prospect and soon Flora went up to change for dinner. She was very thoughtful as she entered the room that had always been hers ever since she had come to live with the Wyldes. It was quite a large room, pleasantly furnished, and until Jane Wylde's marriage to a Venetian nobleman, they had shared it. She thought with a deep sense of thankfulness of the reaction that Mrs Wylde had shown to her disgrace. She resolved to be as helpful as she could whilst she remained at the vicarage, and to co-operate with whatever scheme her protectress might produce for her future employment.

It was while she was unpacking the contents of her bag (for members of the vicarage household were encouraged to look after themselves) that she came upon the still-unopened package from Lord Craythorne. She had had enough money to pay for her short journey on the stage and she had not wanted to discover what the earl might feel she deserved after her bad conduct. Now that Mrs Wylde had received her with kindness she felt a little braver and resolutely she opened the package. Inside was a bank draft for twenty pounds and five sovereigns. Flora looked at them in amazement. This was far in excess of what was due to her, for she had been paid for six months work in arrears only three months before, and moreover, many employers would have considered themselves quite justified in turning her out without a penny. With the draft was a short note which read thus:

I trust that the sum of money enclosed will prove satisfactory. Under the circumstances, I do not feel able to write a character reference for you, but the enclosed letter might prove useful.

Craythorne

Flora picked up the third item in the package, a folded sheet of paper addressed 'To the future employers of Miss Flora Chayter'. She opened it and read these lines:

Miss Flora Chayter was governess to my niece Catherine for just over a year. In that time, Catherine's attitude improved and her understanding increased considerably. I consider Miss Chayter to be a very able teacher.

Craythorne

He had been generous, there was no doubt about it. Her thoughts were interrupted by a soft tap on the door and Mrs Wylde came in with a gown over her arm.

'I only came to bring you a gown of Jane's which I have had pressed for you, as you would not have all your belongings with you as yet.'

Wordlessly, Flora handed her the contents of the package.

'Generous,' she said, echoing Flora's own thought when she saw the bank draft and the money. 'But then, that is like him.'

Flora was too busy thinking about her own situation at the time; later, she would reflect with curiosity about that remark. Mrs Wylde read the letter for future employers carefully, then said diffidently, 'Flora my dear, I have no doubt that Leigh has done his best – and plenty would not have given you any kind of reference at all – but you must see that it is worse than useless.' She sat down next to Flora on the bed. 'Any employer will immediately ask about what has been left out – a testimonial regarding your character – and why.' Seeing Flora looking downcast again, Mrs Wylde went on briskly, 'Cheer up! You have the equivalent of nine months' salary for three months' work and I am sure that something will turn up. Now dress yourself for dinner. I am longing to see if Jane's gowns fit you as well as once they did. Do you remember how you used to be exchanging clothes all the time?'

The upstairs maid gave Flora all the help she needed with fastening the gown, leaving her a little time for reflection. She had every confidence in Mrs Wylde's ability to find her a post. After all, although she lived a retired life, she had many contacts in the polite world. So, too, did Lord Craythorne, however. Furthermore, because they had grown up together, it might follow that they also shared many acquaintances. Anyone contacted by Mrs Wylde could easily find out from the earl about the disgraceful behaviour of Miss Flora Chayter before they even employed her.

These thoughts were not pleasant, and Flora was glad when she was ready, and able to go downstairs to the small drawing-room and wait for dinner. The Revd Peter Wylde was there, having spent the hours before dinner visiting the sick, and he greeted Flora with great pleasure. He was much the same height as Malcolm Brenner, and just as handsome, but here the similarity ended. Whereas Mr Brenner was fair, almost as fair as Flora herself, Mr Wylde had dark-brown hair touched with silver and his eyes were hazel rather than blue. His high brow spoke intelligence, and although his mouth was more frequently serious than Mr Brenner's, his smiles when they came, were warm and sincere. Flora suddenly realized that sincerity was not a quality that came to mind when she thought of Malcolm's expression. As she allowed Mr Wylde to take her hands she reflected that if she had learned to be less easily taken in by a plausible rogue, then that would be something. It was just a great pity that the lesson had had to be learned at such a cost. Although she could now see Malcolm for what he was, there was still an ache in her heart at the loss that she had suffered.

The conversation at dinner was not as awkward as might have been expected. Unlike his wife, Mr Wylde only knew Lord Craythorne and his sister slightly, and so had no enquiries of a personal nature to make. A profound scholar, it had been he who had discovered Flora's quick intellect, and had taught her both Latin and Greek. Now he was very interested to hear how Catherine was progressing in her studies, and whether she had begun to learn one of the ancient languages. Flora was able to answer all of these questions to his satisfaction. If in her heart there was an ache at the thought that she would not be able to supervise her former pupil's future progress, then she managed to conceal it.

'Well, it is a great blessing that you have such an agreeable post,' said the vicar at last, after he had dabbed his lips with his napkin. 'Catherine will need your services for several years yet.' Both the ladies were still eating, and gave their full attention to their last spoonfuls of pudding. 'Then of course,' he went on happily, 'it may be that Lord Craythorne will wish to be married himself before long. I believe he was engaged at one time, was he not? He will surely wish to secure the succession. If he sets up his nursery, Flora, he may well want you to teach his own children, after he has seen what you have been doing at his sister's house.'

'All things are possible,' said Mrs Wylde with a smile. 'Now Flora, shall we leave Peter to his glass of brandy?'

Thankfully Flora agreed. Teach His Lordship's children after he had seen what she had been doing? She could think of more likely contingencies.

Chapter Four

Living once again at the Wyldes' pleasant country vicarage came as welcome balm to Flora's wounded spirit. She had been hit harder by Malcolm's faithlessness than she had admitted to Mrs Wylde. Although she now acknowledged to herself that she had been drawn to him mainly because she had been starved of company of her own age, she was forced to admit that she had been flattered by the attentions of a handsome man and had fallen a little in love with him. She had always been accustomed to think of herself as being quick of apprehension, and an able teacher and student, and she had taken pride in her achievements with Catherine. Her self-confidence had received a heavy blow, both from Malcolm's defection and from her dismissal. It came as a great relief to become once more a cherished member of the household, treated as a much-loved daughter, and with the freedom to be able to read, play music, and draw on her own account, and not just because she was employed to teach these things. She knew that such an existence could not go on indefinitely, but she was human enough to enjoy it for the time being.

Deep down inside, however, there was a vein of anxiety – the fear that however hard Mrs Wylde might try to secure employment for her, such a post would not be beyond the reach of Lord Craythorne and his bad opinion of her. Meantime, the day when Mrs Wylde was due to set out for Venice was drawing nearer and something would have to be settled by then, for it would not be proper for Flora to remain in the vicarage unchaperoned.

Soon after Flora's arrival, it had become necessary to tell the vicar that she had left her employment for good.

'But . . . but what did you say?' faltered Flora. She was fond of both the Wyldes and longed for their good opinion, but she knew that Mr Wylde set very high standards and would look unfavourably on any hint of immorality.

'I simply told him that Maria had taken a sudden and unreasoning dislike to you,' said Mrs Wylde. It was a warm sunny day, and the ladies were engaged in the pleasant occupation of picking flowers. The vicar's wife carefully selected a bloom and snipped it off with her scissors. 'I have often spoken to him about her foolish fancies, so he is grieved but does not blame you. However, I would advise you to avoid the subject of the Brenners and all their connections. Flora, do put that poor flower in my basket. You must have been holding it for a full minute!'

Flora said nothing to the vicar about her former employer and her family, and she suspected that he had been given the same warning, for he did not raise the matter again. It simply confirmed what Flora had always known: that although Mr Wylde was a strong leader of his flock and looked up to and respected in the parish, it was his helpmeet who made most of the decisions about family life.

The following day as the two women were engaged in sewing for the poor-basket, Mrs Wylde said to Flora, 'My dear, I have been wondering whether in our search for further employment for you we are casting our net over too narrow an area. Would you object to a post of companion rather than that of governess?'

Flora enjoyed teaching and her heart sank a little at the

thought of being at the beck and call of some crotchety old lady, but she was very conscious of her obligation to the Wylde family, so she willingly said, 'I should not mind at all. I should be very happy to find any occupation.'

'Then I shall write to Miss Bridgeworth,' replied her companion. 'As you know, she is to accompany me on my journey to Rome, and I do not think that she has yet been able to make arrangements for a companion for her sister whilst she is away. Would you be willing to take up such a position, Flora? It would only be temporary, but it would be something, and it would give you a chance to look about you for other things. Then when Miss Bridgeworth returns, she will be able to provide you with a reference which hopefully will be of more use to you than the one that Leigh wrote.'

'Why, of course, I will go to her if required,' answered Flora as she fastened off her thread. 'Pray tell her that I will be more than happy to do so if needed.'

No more was said about the matter until a week later, when a letter arrived for Mrs Wylde. She opened it at the breakfast table, glanced through its contents, gave a sigh that could have been one of satisfaction, or of vexation, looked quickly at Flora then turned to her husband and said, 'I would appreciate the opportunity of speaking privately with you in your study after breakfast, my dear, if you should be free.' Mr Wylde gave his assent. 'Then perhaps you would take the provisions that we decided upon to the Ramsden family,' went on the vicar's wife, speaking this time to Flora. 'I should like them to have them as soon as possible.'

Flora agreed readily and went upstairs to put on her bonnet. She had always enjoyed being involved in the task of caring for the people of the village. It would be a wrench to give it up when she had to move on. She could only hope that Miss Bridgeworth might be charitably inclined, and willing to allow her new companion to help her in her work.

She enjoyed her visit to the Ramsdens' tiny cottage. At leisure times – which were few – it was full to overflowing with Ramsdens of all shapes and sizes. Now it would be fuller still, as Mrs Ramsden had just been brought to bed with a new baby. Mrs Ramsden was very grateful for all that Mrs Wylde had sent her, and insisted on getting up to make Flora a cup of tea.

'A visit from the vicarage is always welcome,' she said, 'and I've a bit of good news for Mrs Wylde if you'll be so good as to give it to her, miss; well, more than one bit, really.'

'Of course,' replied Flora who was fully occupied with holding the baby whilst Mrs Ramsden put the kettle on.

'There's been two poachers who've been coming onto Sir Alan's land and causing trouble for some time, miss. Well, Ramsden caught them last week and Sir Alan was so pleased that he's paying him a bit more a week; and he's spoke to his housekeeper, and she's agreed to take our Betty on in the kitchens. So what with our Robbie going into the Navy, that's two less mouths to feed, and a bit more to go round as well!'

'You must be so pleased, Mrs Ramsden,' said Flora. She thought guiltily of how much she was enjoying her leisure time. How much leisure would Betty get? She resolved to be much more thankful for all that she had.

On her arrival back at the vicarage she immediately sensed an air of suppressed excitement. Mrs Wylde came hurrying into the hall to greet her, obviously trying hard not to smile too much.

'Go upstairs straight away, my dear, and put off your cloak and bonnet, and do be quick! I have something very important that I wish to say to you!'

'Yes, of course, Aunt Letty,' replied Flora, catching something of her mood and hurrying up the stairs. Once they were together in the drawing-room, Mrs Wylde began without any preliminaries.

'I have had a letter from Miss Bridgeworth!' she said, her eyes sparkling.

'And she says she will have me! How splendid!' replied Flora, trying hard to feel as pleased as she knew she should. 'When should I pack, ma'am?'

'Ah,' said Mrs Wylde, and she sat down rubbing her lip thoughtfully. 'That is not exactly what she says.' Flora waited expectantly. 'My friend Miss Bridgeworth, as I believe I mentioned before, resides with her sister to whom you were to have been companion – as I hoped. However, in her letter she tells me that as her sister is in poor health, she has thought about the matter again, and has decided that she would be too anxious to leave her.' To Flora's surprise, her protectress looked if anything a little triumphant.

'So you have no companion for your journey,' said Flora slowly. 'What will you do?'

'On the contrary,' replied Mrs Wylde, smiling mysteriously. 'I think that I may have found the perfect travelling companion.' In the silence that followed her words, the ticking of the little clock on the drawing-room mantelpiece could be heard quite clearly.

'Me?' whispered Flora at last. As if the sound of her voice had broken a spell, Mrs Wylde got up hastily and rushed over to Flora's chair to take her by the hands and pull Flora to her feet.

'Of course you!' she exclaimed. 'Who better? What do I want with fussy old Miss Bridgeworth when I can take Flora?' Seeing her young companion was dumbstruck she said concernedly, 'What is wrong? You do want to travel, don't you?'

'Of course I do!' exclaimed Flora. 'But it seems so unfair that I should be dismissed for bad behaviour, and then rewarded for it!'

'Nonsense!' returned her companion. 'You will be coming because I need you, and if you enjoy yourself as well, so much the better. Now stop dwelling on what is over and done with. Think about seeing Jane and her new baby instead.'

'Oh Aunt Letty, are you sure you want me?' asked Flora anxiously.

'My dear, I couldn't be more delighted! And now that it is settled, we can make lists of what we need to take. Bring pen and paper and we will start straight away.'

Later, after Flora had returned with writing materials, she ventured to say, 'There is a further advantage that perhaps you had not considered, ma'am.'

'And what might that be?' asked Mrs Wylde.

'Well, I shall be gone so long that Lord Craythorne may well forget all about me.' Mrs Wylde bent over the pens that Flora had brought and carefully selected one.

'At any rate, he may have changed his mind about you by then,' she said, without looking up from her task. 'Now, clothes first! Fortunately, the things that Jane left here will almost fit you, and in that we can make a virtue of necessity for I have been reliably informed that obviously new things can often be confiscated by Customs.'

The next three weeks were very busy ones for both ladies. The gowns that Jane had left were found to be not quite such a good fit as Mrs Wylde had predicted, for Flora was a little thinner than Jane, and everything needed taking in. There was work to be done on Mrs Wylde's clothes, too, and a number of household tasks to be performed so that everything would be in perfect order when they left.

The vicar accepted all the bustle that was going on with commendable stoicism, and spent much of the day in his study when he was not visiting his parishioners. He was not going to be idle during their absence. A friend of his who was a professor at Oxford was coming to stay with him and they were going to write a book together on the works of Josephus.

'Really, my dear, I sometimes think that you cannot wait to

get us out of the house,' said his wife one day at dinner about a week before they were due to depart. 'It is not very flattering.'

'Perhaps so,' replied the vicar, his eyes twinkling. 'But then you are no less eager to be gone.'

'Only because I am so excited at the thought of seeing Jane. She will be sorry to miss you.'

Mr Wylde's eyes clouded for a moment.

'And I will be sorry to miss her,' he said regretfully. 'Even so, I cannot put off this work any longer. Perhaps we can go again some time. It is too long since I viewed the ancient sites. If you see anything of interest. . . .'

'I will bring it back if it is removable, or sketch it if it isn't,' promised his wife fondly.

'I should have thought to have asked Craythorne the same thing,' went on Mr Wylde. 'I believe that he was quite a good scholar.'

At the sound of Craythorne's name Flora swallowed a piece of fruit hastily and started to choke. Mrs Wylde busied herself with finding water for her, and by the time she had regained her composure, it was time for the ladies to leave the vicar to the single glass of brandy which was all he allowed himself.

'What did Uncle Peter mean about Lord Craythorne?' she asked once they were settled in the drawing-room. 'Why did he mention him?'

Mrs Wylde started to extract a tangled length of thread from her work basket, carefully avoiding Flora's gaze.

'It is simply that Peter remembers Lord Craythorne's love of the Continent. He has travelled there a number of times since he first made the Grand Tour as a young man. I expect that Peter is regretful that he has no one more knowledgeable than myself to look out for the artefacts on which he has set his heart.' She paused for a moment, then still with her eyes on her work basket, she went on, 'I understand that Leigh is to make another tour soon – perhaps even at the same time as ourselves.'

Flora turned pale and dropped her own sewing. 'Oh no!' she exclaimed.

'Flora, my dear, you are being absurd,' answered Mrs Wylde as she bent down to help Flora retrieve her work. 'The man has just as much right to travel on the Continent as do we.'

Flora sighed. 'Of course you are right, Aunt Letty. Even if he is travelling at the same time as we are, that does not mean that we need ever meet him at all. He may not be interested in the same places, for one thing.'

'Very true, my dear. But to get back to the artefacts, it has occurred to me that you will be able to guide me, for you have benefited directly from Peter's scholarship from your childhood.'

Flora looked doubtful. 'I will do what I can,' she said. 'But I cannot pretend to be an expert.'

'I am sure you will be a great help,' said the other. 'And of course we shall have Mr Warren to help us too.'

'Mr Warren?' queried Flora.

'He is the gentleman who is to accompany us to Venice,' explained Mrs Wylde. 'We cannot travel all that way without an escort, you know.'

'Yes, I know,' replied Flora. 'But foolishly, I had not given the matter any thought. Who is Mr Warren, and why have you not mentioned him before?'

Mrs Wylde laid down her sewing and looked up at her. 'You will understand why I did not mention it earlier when I tell you that Mr Warren is Lord Craythorne's secretary. It appears that he has to go to Venice on his employer's account so he will be able to go with us.'

Flora smiled faintly.

'I suppose that is why you said a little while ago that Lord Craythorne might change his mind about me,' she said. 'You meant that Mr Warren would be able to speak favourably of me, did you not?'

'That was part of my idea certainly,' responded Mrs Wylde. At that moment, the door opened to admit the vicar. 'Ah, there you are, my dear,' she said to her husband. 'Would you be so good as to ring for tea?'

Chapter Five

'Please do not be alarmed when Mr Warren appears,' Mrs Wylde had said to Flora, 'but I am afraid he looks a little like Lord Craythorne. They are distant cousins, you see, on Leigh's father's side.'

Flora was very glad of the warning, for when she first caught sight of Mr Warren at a distance, he could easily have been mistaken for the earl. Close observation showed him to be much the same height, but somewhat more finely drawn, more slender, with hair that was not quite so dark or so curly, and rather less prominent features. It seemed to Flora as if the two men were different paintings of the same subject: the earl done in oils, and his cousin in water-colours; or perhaps one might even say that the earl was the rough sketch, his cousin the finished article.

Despite his likeness to Craythorne – and Flora was relieved to note the absence of those lowering brows – he seemed perfectly affable. Not that she had much chance for speech with him, for from the moment of his arrival, Mrs Wylde seemed to find a hundred and one tasks for her to do, which only seemed to be finished when they were ready to get into the carriage to be off. There was a moment's delay, as Mr Wylde wondered whether it would be sensible for him to come with them to Dover.

'Then you know, my love, I could have a word with—'

Mrs Wylde, hastily put a finger on his lips. 'Now, my dear, do not tease yourself,' said his wife. 'You know that Mr Warren has our welfare in hand and will certainly deal with the innkeeper and harbour master for us. Moreover, who can tell whether Professor Adams might not decide to arrive today? How dreadful it would be if you were not here to welcome him!'

'Oh, yes; very well then, my dear, you know best,' he said. 'Good-bye, both of you and God bless you.'

'There!' declared Mrs Wylde with satisfaction, sitting back in her seat with what could only be described as an inelegant flop after the last frantic wave as they turned the corner out of Vicarage Lane. 'Thank goodness that's over.' Flora looked a little surprised at her pleasure. There had always been a strong bond of affection between the vicar and his wife that encompassed the whole of their household. Mrs Wylde flushed a little and straightened. 'I beg your pardon, my dear. Please do not think that I am glad to leave Peter, for it is quite otherwise, I assure you. In fact, I hate leave-taking so much that I am relieved that it is over. You must admit that we have been very busy these past few days; I am really quite thankful to stop all that packing and just let the carriage take me along.'

They were alone together inside, as Mr Warren was riding alongside on a horse that looked very like one that Flora had seen in Craythorne's possession. It seemed that even their taste in horseflesh was similar. Mrs Wylde had brought no abigail with her. She and Flora had agreed that they would be able to do everything necessary for each other during the journey. The abigail, who had originally agreed to come most reluctantly, was delighted to be relieved of the need to go and was to stay behind on a visit to her married sister on half pay until Mrs Wylde returned.

They had set off in good time. Mr Warren had travelled up

from Dover the previous day, and had spent the night with a relative. Flora had a nasty feeling that this must have been her former employer, but she did not ask. He had come on to the vicarage first thing, arriving at nine o'clock, and bearing them off as soon afterwards as their preparations would allow.

Apparently, when Mr Warren had left Dover the previous day it had been ideal crossing weather and he was hoping that they would be able to catch the tide on their return. They made one brief stop in order to change the horses and have something to eat. Flora was very much hoping that Mr Warren was not one of those men who have to talk endlessly about their work and their employer. She still did not feel up to hearing paeans of praise about Lord Craythorne. Thankfully he did not refer to the earl at all during their simple repast of bread, cheese and soup, but confined his conversation to the weather and other general topics. Flora wondered whether Mrs Wylde had cautioned him as to the subjects of his conversation out of consideration for her feelings.

As the journey went on, she also found herself wondering what Lord Craythorne would do without his secretary for so many months. Suddenly she recalled something that the vicar had said not long after she had arrived.

'Was Lord Craythorne really engaged at one time?' she asked her companion. Mrs Wylde started, for the silence that had fallen upon the two of them had been quite a protracted one, and she had nearly nodded off to sleep.

'What was that, my dear? Leigh engaged? What are you talking about?'

Flora coloured for no reason that she could imagine.

'I was just remembering how Uncle Peter had said that he thought the earl might marry soon. To tell the truth, I was wondering how he would manage without Mr Warren, then thought that perhaps he would be concerned with more personal matters.'

'As far as I know, he has no plans to marry at present. If you want up-to-date news of society, then Peter is not the one to consult. Leigh was engaged some time ago, but the whole thing was broken off. I do not know the details, but I believe that Leigh was the wronged party in the case.'

Making every allowance for the partiality of long acquaintance, Flora drew her own conclusions. She could not imagine any female getting the better of Lord Craythorne.

They made good time on the journey, arriving in the early afternoon, and found that Mr Warren's hopes were realized. There was a fine light breeze and the day was sunny.

'We'll have a following wind,' said Mr Warren delightedly. 'That will make our journey all the quicker. We may even be there in under three hours! Just think of that!'

'I had rather think of a comfortable lodging,' said Mrs Wylde looking longingly towards the inn. 'Must we really travel on today?'

'Certainly,' replied Mr Warren as he helped them down from the coach. 'We are very fortunate to be able to set off like this. It has been known for travellers to have to endure weeks of delay here.'

'Well, we certainly don't want that, do we, Flora?'

'No indeed,' agreed Flora fervently. 'Which ship are we to board, Mr Warren?'

'*The Fair Maid* – look, over there,' he replied, pointing. With his dark curls blowing about his face, he looked more like his kinsman than ever, and Flora barely repressed a shudder. He escorted them to the gangplank which led onto a very serviceable ship and handed them into the care of a stout, good-humoured-looking sailor.

'I will attend to the luggage and make sure that everything has been collected from the inn. This fellow will show you to your quarters.'

The ladies thanked him and then followed the sailor down

the companion way and into a small cabin in which there were two bunks.

'Saloon's at the end,' he said.

'Will there be anything to eat?' asked Mrs Wylde hopefully.

'Not much to speak of, mum,' he answered. 'But the lad might get you a cup of tea an' mebbe some bread and butter, if'n you ask.'

'Thank you,' said Mrs Wylde. As the cabin door closed she looked around her and said, 'It's a good thing we aren't here for long. There isn't much room, is there?'

'I don't suppose there can be,' replied Flora. 'Not on board ship, I mean. Shall we go and look for that tea?'

The boy in the dining-room was just as obliging as his crew-mate had predicted and in no time, the ladies were enjoying a cup of tea and some bread and butter and cakes as well.

Not long after they had consumed this light repast, the increased movement of the ship told them that they were getting underway. Suddenly, Flora realized that the adventure had really begun. The coach ride in itself had not seemed particularly exciting, but this was her very first sea voyage.

'Oh Aunt Letty, we have actually started!' she exclaimed, her eyes shining. 'Can we go up on deck?'

There was no immediate response from Mrs Wylde, who had suddenly turned rather pale.

'You may do so, of course, Flora,' she replied. 'But pray hold me excused. I really feel that I would like to retire to the cabin and lie down.'

'But of course,' said Flora, in quick concern. 'I will come with you and. . . .'

Mrs Wylde shook her head and made a slight gesture with her hand.

'As far as the cabin door,' she insisted. 'Then leave me if you please. I had rather be on my own.'

'If you are sure,' replied Flora as they made their way to the door. The boat rocked a little more, and Flora could not help but cry out, 'Oh ma'am, I do believe we are in the open sea!'

'I dare say,' responded her companion as tartly as she was able. 'Oh well, the sooner we are out there, the sooner we will be in France.'

'That's right,' said Flora soothingly. 'Perhaps even in less than three hours, Mr Warren said. Now lie down and try to sleep.'

'Thank you, Flora,' murmured Mrs Wylde as she lay down on the lower bunk. 'Would you mind just passing me that basin?'

Flora was very thankful to escape the tiny cabin. She was delighted to discover that she appeared to be a good sailor, but was not sure whether the sight and sound of someone being ill would make her feel less resilient. Quickly she made her way on deck. Already, Dover was beginning to recede behind them. The breeze seemed stronger than on land, and she was glad of the warm cloak that she had 'inherited' from Jane. Carefully she tied the strings of her bonnet in a double bow. The waves were quite small with white tops and the clouds scudded swiftly across the sky. It looked as if Mr Warren would be right.

At first, she thought that the deck was deserted, but looking across to the other side, she could see their escort gazing out to sea. He had put on a dark grey cloak to protect himself against the wind and the spray, and his hair, no longer confined by a ribbon, was blowing about his shoulders in wild disarray. She made her way over to him, but at the last moment, a wave that was larger than usual tossed the boat a little more, and Flora found herself flung against him. Automatically, he put out an arm to save her, clamping her to him with a strength that surprised her.

'Oh thank you,' she cried, laughing a little because she was so excited about the adventure. Then she looked up at him and the laugh died on her lips, for she found herself clasped not in the arms of Matthew Warren, but of his formidable kinsman, Lord Craythorne.

It would be hard to say who was the more astonished. For a moment or two, they stood transfixed, then, as realization dawned, Flora saw the earl's heavy black brows draw together in that familiar expression of disapproval, but with something else added, which Flora could not define until he said contemptuously as he released her, 'I am sorry to disappoint you, Miss Chayter. You were expecting some other man, no doubt.'

Flora did not immediately take in the implications of his words. When she did so, her face flushed angrily.

'I certainly was not expecting you, My Lord,' she answered. 'I will intrude upon your solitude no longer.' She took a hasty step backwards, and instantly Craythorne made as if to pursue her. Flora was not thinking clearly and, in her panic, she thought that he meant to strike her. She put up her arm defensively, took another step back and found herself seized for the second time.

'Have some sense, woman,' exclaimed the earl. 'Look where you're going on board ship.' He turned her round and pointed to a coil of rope over which she would certainly have fallen had he not prevented it. 'What the devil are you doing here, anyway?' he went on.

Flora drew herself up with as much dignity as was possible on the deck of a moving ship.

'That is none of your concern, My Lord,' she said. 'I am no longer, thank God, answerable to you for my actions, and may do as I please.'

As an exit line it could not have been better. The sea, too, was kind to Flora and restrained its lively motion for long enough to allow her to escape the earl's presence with dignity. She hurried back to her cabin to avoid any further encounter with him. On arriving there, she discovered that Mrs Wylde had fallen into a doze, so she could not tell her about what had happened, or question her about why Lord Craythorne might be travelling on the same vessel.

She looked regretfully out of the tiny porthole. She would far rather have been on deck than in this cabin whose air, truth to tell, smelled a little sour, but she could not risk meeting him again. As to his purposes, she could only suppose that as Mrs Wylde had suggested earlier that week, he had decided to visit the Continent again. Maybe since he had loaned Mrs Wylde his secretary as an escort, he had decided to use Mr Warren's absence as an excuse for going on a journey of his own. She could only hope that once they arrived at Calais, his route would take him in a different direction. How embarrassing, though, to have met him in such a way!

There was a small chair in the cabin, and sitting down Flora found it to be surprisingly comfortable. She had in her reticule a book of poems which she took out in order to reread some of Shakespeare's sonnets. Having read through her favourite 'Let me not to the marriage of true minds admit impediments' – she closed her eyes to see whether she could still recite it off by heart, and was pleased to discover that her memory was as good as ever. After she had gone through it in her mind, she sat thinking about one or two of the lines that were in it. Shakespeare had written that love was 'an ever fixed mark, that looks on tempests and is never shaken'. Malcolm Brenner had basely deserted her at the very first hint of a cloud on the horizon.

Suddenly Flora realized that she was completely cured of her love for him. A relationship that could not stand up to the difficulties that life might throw in its path was not worth having. Maybe she would never find someone whom she could love and who would love her in that steadfast way, but she knew now that she would never settle for second best. Perhaps she could set up a small school instead when they returned from the

Continent. Flora drifted into a happy daydream, and was surprised when a change in the motion of the ship roused her and she discovered that she had actually been asleep. Looking out of the porthole she was amazed to see the coast, and realized that they had nearly arrived.

Mrs Wylde was still asleep, so Flora roused her gently. The older lady still looked alarmingly pale, and clutching Flora's hand, she said, 'Oh my dear, are we there indeed?'

'I believe so, Aunt Letty,' replied Flora. 'Shall I go and find out what is happening?'

Hardly had she spoken, when there was a tap on the door. Flora's heart skipped a beat as she remembered Lord Craythorne, and wondered illogically whether he might have come to berate her. She opened it to reveal his unalarming cousin on the threshold.

'I'm afraid the packet cannot get into the harbour,' he said, so apologetically that one might almost have supposed it to be his personal fault. 'The sea is too rough and the tide too low.'

Flora would not have thought it possible for Mrs Wylde to get any paler, but that lady proved her wrong.

'Oh no!' she declared faintly. 'I refuse to sail back to Dover!'

Mr Warren smiled sympathetically.

'No indeed, ma'am, that will not be necessary, or even possible, given the quarter in which the wind is sitting. But I am afraid that you will have to step into a rowing boat in order to get ashore.'

Judging that Mrs Wylde would be best served if she could be hurried into a boat without having too much time to think about it, Flora started to bustle about, getting her companion's things together.

'Thank you, ma'am,' said Mr Warren gratefully catching her eye. 'Please be up on deck as soon as you can.'

He had disappeared before Flora had remembered that she wanted to ask him what he knew about the presence of his kinsman, and then she had enough to think about with bundling the rather tottery rector's wife into her cloak, tying her bonnet strings firmly and making sure that she had her reticule.

'You are a wonder,' said Mrs Wylde gratefully as they left the cabin. 'Miss Bridgeworth would not have been half as valuable to me, I am sure.'

Once on deck they could see that the shore still looked to be quite a distance away and that a little group of fishing boats were making their way to the packet in order to relieve it of its passengers and cargo. One fishing boat was already tied alongside. It looked an alarmingly long way down the side of the packet to the little boat below, but Flora did not draw Mrs Wylde's attention to this, choosing instead to encourage her to take deep breaths of fresh air.

'You were quite right, Flora,' she said, a little colour beginning to return to her cheeks. 'Perhaps I would have been better on deck.'

A lady standing nearby heard this remark and spoke to Mrs Wylde, leaving Flora free to observe what was going on. There appeared to be some kind of altercation taking place between one of the crew of the packet and a Frenchman in the boat below. Carried out in some kind of patois, it could possibly have been part of an ongoing argument and was quite beyond Flora's ability to understand. Mr Warren appeared at her side, having arranged for the conveyance of their baggage.

'What is the delay?' she asked him. 'Can you understand what they are saying?'

'No indeed,' he laughed. 'But I believe it is to do with a never-ending dispute between the boatmen and those coming into the harbour. The Frenchmen want to be paid for rowing passengers to the shore.'

'Well, that seems reasonable,' said Flora mildly.

'Yes, but at two guineas a boatload? We could have hired a packet for five,' he replied.

'That is excessive,' she agreed. 'What happens now?'

Mr Warren shrugged. 'We are at their mercy,' he admitted. 'We can argue as much as we like, but they have the boats and we cannot get ashore without them.'

He was right, of course, but Flora could not help feeling that his attitude was a little defeatist.

At that moment, a raucous shout rang out from the side of the packet, and a little above them. Flora looked up to see Lord Craythorne perched precariously on the side of the vessel, hanging on to a rope which was wrapped several times around his arm, and calling down to the men below. With his wild black hair and casually assured stance he looked every inch a pirate.

There was an answering shout from the boat below and another conversation ensued, this time in idiomatic French, of which Flora only understood a handful of words, fluent as she was. Eventually after roars of laughter on both sides, Craythorne sprang down.

'Lower away,' he said to the crewman standing ready alongside the lifting gear. Flora and Mrs Wylde were in the first boat with Matthew Warren, the lady to whom they had spoken on deck and her husband. Mr Warren gamely volunteered to be the first to be lowered on the very frail-looking seat and the ladies were very thankful to see him there in the boat below ready to receive them. Flora, by dint of much coaxing and encouragement persuaded Mrs Wylde to go next, then did the same for the other lady whose assurance seemed to have deserted her in face of this adventure. Flora then followed herself. She could not help but wonder from whom she might have inherited this taste for new experiences, for the sea voyage had not daunted her, and this present adventure she found novel and not at all unpleasant.

When they were some little distance away from the packet, she caught sight of Lord Craythorne standing beside a female figure, his arm around her, and she found herself wondering who might be accompanying him on his journey. Certainly the lady with him would need to descend to a fishing boat by means of that tiny seat, but Flora found it quite impossible to imagine the earl doing so. He would be far more likely to swing himself down on the end of that rope. The sight of his female companion cheered Flora greatly. Surely if he had brought a mistress he would be most unlikely to inflict himself upon their party. His presence on the same boat must be nothing more than a ghastly coincidence.

The short journey from the packet to the shore was not particularly pleasant. The grey-green water of the choppy sea seemed alarmingly close and the very insouciance of the sailors was unnerving. In the little fishing boat, they seemed to be much more conscious of the wind, and consequently felt colder. In addition to this, the fishing boat had quite a lot of water slopping about in the bottom, making it a matter of considerable importance as to where one put one's feet. Mrs Wylde did not enjoy this part of the journey either, and Flora found herself patting her hand and saying soothing words just to get the time on, rather than discussing the presence of Lord Craythorne. Seeing him again when she had hoped never to do so had made her feel almost morbidly superstitious. It was as if saying his name might mean that she would encounter him once more in even more embarrassing circumstances. Furthermore, the presence of the other couple in the boat made personal conversations impossible.

Fortunately the trip did not take nearly as long as expected and soon they were being helped to shore by Mr Warren. Both ladies felt a little alarmed at the way that the land seemed to move beneath their feet, but Mr Warren assured them that this was quite normal.

'You'll soon get your land . . . er . . . limbs back, ladies,' he said. 'There is a short walk to the inn, or I can send for a conveyance if you prefer.' They both declared that the walk would be a welcome change after all their travelling. Now that she was on land, Mrs Wylde was recovering her complexion and with it much of her sensible country-woman's demeanour and pronounced herself to be ready for anything.

'As long as "anything" includes something to eat,' she said frankly. 'And no wonder we are starving, for I see it is five o'clock! Let us start immediately.' Mr Warren looked apologetic.

'Unfortunately we will have to visit the Custom House first,' he murmured.

'The Custom House?' exclaimed Mrs Wylde.

'Why yes, ma'am. They will wish to search us and our belongings for contraband goods; and new items may be confiscated.'

'Disgraceful!' declared Mrs Wylde. 'I am not a smuggler and I would defy anyone to say that I am.' Flora could see that this robust attitude was unlikely to find favour with pompous, petty and probably corrupt officials and she looked at Mr Warren anxiously.

'Pray, ma'am,' he began, but before he could say more, he was touched on the arm by a respectable man who had come from the direction of the Custom House.

'*M'sieur* Warren?' he enquired politely. Warren nodded. '*Pardon, m'sieur, mesdames,*' he said with a little bow. 'My name is Henri Corbieux, and I 'ave been engaged to – 'ow you say – guide you on your journey. If you will please to follow me. . . .'

'But we need to go to the Customs, I believe,' said Mr Warren.

'That is not necessary. Matters 'ave been arranged. Please?' He gestured once more that they should go with him.

'Well, it appears that we can go straight to the inn,' he said, relief clearly written across his brow. 'Shall we go, ladies?'

Relieved at not having to steer Mrs Wylde away from a confrontation with French officials which she would certainly have lost and which would probably have left them the poorer, Flora willingly accompanied Mr Warren and the little Frenchman. The latter's assistance would certainly make matters easier, but Flora could not help but wonder why Mr Warren had seemed unaware of his presence until he actually turned up. She glanced back at the packet. There was no sign of Craythorne. Flora supposed, with a sigh, that it would be too much to hope that he was so disgusted with the idea of sharing the Continent with her that he had decided to go straight home.

M Corbieux led them efficiently to the Hôtel D'Angleterre which proved to be an excellent inn under the able control of one M Dessin who greeted them himself, hoped they would have a pleasant stay, and assured them of his most courteous attention. Dinner, he promised them, would be ready in an hour by which time he hoped that all their party would be assembled.

'For, *madame*,' he assured Mrs Wylde, as he conducted them himself to their chambers, 'I have often had the honour of serving My Lord, and I am overjoyed that he is honouring my house again and with so charming a company too.'

The sudden discovery of the earl's presence amongst their company came to Flora like a blow to the stomach. She actually halted on the stairs, so it was a mercy that no one was immediately following her, and for a moment she felt almost as faint as she had done on hearing of Malcolm's desertion. The sight of Mrs Wylde's figure ascending in front of her brought her to her senses, as she realized that her kind protectress must almost certainly also be her betrayer. Swiftly she pulled herself together and caught up with the others.

Flora and Mrs Wylde were to share a room, and no sooner had the door shut behind them than Flora turned to the older lady, the light of battle in her eye.

'Now, ma'am, a straight answer if you please. Are we or are we not travelling in company with Lord Craythorne?'

Mrs Wylde looked at her, coloured, turned away and began to say, 'Well, my dear. . . .' It was all the confirmation that Flora needed.

'Aunt Letty, how could you!' she exclaimed in disbelief and outrage. 'When I saw him on board the ship, I supposed his presence to be some sort of a horrible coincidence. I never dreamed that you. . . .' Her voice tailed off.

'I must say, Flora,' began Letty now thoroughly on the defensive, 'that I have every right to travel in company with a gentleman of my acquaintance, if I am properly chap—' Realizing the infelicitous nature of her comment, she stopped in mid-sentence.

'Chaperoned!' finished Flora for her. 'Yes,ma'am, I see. Your friend could not come and so lacking the essential female companion you pretended that you wanted me' – and here her voice trembled a little – 'and concealed from me the one thing that would have held me back from coming with you – the identity of your escort – until it was too late. You knew that it would be an embarrassment to me but you did it anyway. I believed you to have a greater regard for me.' She turned away, and walked to the window, struggling to hold back the tears of anger and disappointment.

'Flora, no!' cried Mrs Wylde, moving as if to put a hand on Flora's shoulder, but then allowing her hand to drop, judging that perhaps it might not quite be the right moment. 'That was not the way of it at all. Miss Bridgeworth was to come with me, it was true, and I was grateful to her for making my journey possible. But I was not looking forward to several months in her company. I only have to be with her for two minutes and I run out of things to say to her!

'As soon as you came home I realized that you would be free and that I wanted you to be my companion on the tour. I knew that Miss Bridgeworth had only offered to come out of kindness, and not because she wanted to do so. I wrote to her thanking her, but reminding her of how ill her sister could be – in a kind way, of course – and saying how much I appreciated her coming when I knew how anxious she would be all the time we were away. . . .'

'In fact you played on her fears,' remarked Flora without turning round. 'That was not well done.'

'No indeed,' agreed the other lady in subdued tones. 'I do not know what Peter would say if he knew. However, if she was prompted to such anxiety by my letter, how much more concerned would she be across the Channel, receiving no news at all?'

'You have done her a service when one thinks of it,' said Flora ironically.

'Yes, my dear, I think that I have,' replied Mrs Wylde naïvely. 'So she wrote back and excused herself and I was able to claim the companion I wanted. You were the one I chose, Flora.'

Flora turned round to face her. 'That's all very well, ma'am,' she said, 'but it does not explain why you encouraged me to come, knowing that Craythorne and I would be forced to meet. Why, you even wove that story of his plans to visit the Continent as well, so that if I saw him at Dover or on the boat, I would not be suspicious.'

Mrs Wylde looked the picture of guilt. 'What can I do except say that I am very sorry for deceiving you?' she said.

'I'm sure that you are,' replied Flora, 'but that does not alter the fact that this will be embarrassing for us both, for it is plain that the earl was as surprised by my presence as I was by his.' Mrs Wylde hurried over to her now, and dared to catch hold of her arm; Flora did not shake her off as she might have done five minutes before.

'Yes, but Flora, remember what I said! This opportunity to get to know you will be all to the good! By the end of our travels he will realize – he must realize – that he was mistaken in you! And I must tell you that he likes to ride everywhere. We will probably not see him much on the journey because we shall be in the carriage and he will be on horseback; and when we reach places to visit, well, his interests will no doubt take him in different directions altogether. Ten to one, we will hardly see him at all!'

Flora had to smile ruefully, then.

'You really must decide, ma'am, which case you are pleading! Is it that I shan't see him at all, or that I shall see him and make a good impression?'

'Oh Flora, have you stopped being angry with me?' asked Mrs Wylde anxiously. Flora looked at her and recalled that this woman had taken her in when plenty would have turned her from the door.

'I suppose it cannot be helped now,' she sighed. Mrs Wylde sighed too, but with relief.

'In that case, we had better get ready to go downstairs,' she said.

'Downstairs!' exclaimed Flora in outraged tones that would have been more appropriate had Mrs Wylde suggested that they go to the moon. 'But I cannot possibly go downstairs!'

'What about your dinner?' asked her companion. 'It will do you no good to starve yourself.'

'Surely I can have something to eat in my room,' pleaded Flora.

'Well yes,' agreed Mrs Wylde. 'But you will have to face Leigh sometime. Better sooner than later, surely.' After a little more discussion, Flora eventually allowed herself to be persuaded, on condition that Mrs Wylde would agree to explain to His Lordship first how she came to be travelling in the party, and how she had been unaware of his presence until they were on board ship.

'I would give something to be invisibly present when you explain everything to Lord Craythorne,' she said, venturing a gallant attempt at humour.

In the event, there was no need for Flora to wish for any such thing, and unfortunately the kindly covering of invisibility was not granted to her. They both had only a small amount of luggage as the majority would be sealed by the Customs so that it would not be tampered with by other officials before they reached Paris. In consequence they did not make a complete change of clothing, but contented themselves with tidying their hair, (which truth to tell had become very disarranged during the sea passage, despite their bonnets) shaking out their gowns and finding shawls to wear.

As they reached the bottom of the stairs, M Dessin appeared and with much bowing, indicated that they should go into a small private parlour. Courteously he opened the door for them. It was a pleasant room with a good fire burning, but the surroundings made no impact upon them at all, for standing by the window was Lord Craythorne, looking more severe than Flora had ever seen him. He, too, had had time to attend to his appearance. The wild black curls were now neatly confined with a bow, and his linen looked fresh.

'Well?' he said, looking at Mrs Wylde. To Flora, his voice had never sounded more harsh. 'Do you think I might have an explanation?'

'An explanation of what, pray?' asked Mrs Wylde. She made a fair attempt at sounding dignified, but her voice held an undoubted wobble.

'Come, ma'am, don't be so absurd,' he snapped back. 'We arranged that I would escort you to Venice to visit your daughter whilst at the same time undertaking various commissions of my own. You told me that you had arranged for one Miss Bridgeworth – a spinster of fifty – to accompany you. Now I find that instead of Miss Bridgeworth, you have brought Miss Chayter.'

'And what is that to you?' asked Mrs Wylde. 'The identity of my companion, or her age, should surely be a matter of indifference to you.'

'Why certainly,' agreed the earl. 'And so it would have been had you not chosen deliberately to bring someone whom I had ample cause to dismiss from my employ not six weeks ago! I presume you are aware of this fact. Or has Miss Chayter imposed on you as disgracefully as she has imposed upon my family?' Mrs Wylde glanced quickly at Flora. She was looking composed but rather white.

'Certainly not,' she replied, going to the earl's side and laying a hand on his arm. 'Leigh, is it really necessary for Flora to be present whilst we discuss this? It is distressing her.'

Craythorne shook off her hand. 'Is it indeed?' he said, staring at Flora in grim satisfaction. 'Then perhaps there is some justice in the world after all. Considering the distress and inconvenience that she has caused in my sister's household – and in particular to my niece, Catherine – I think it is only fair that she should experience some herself.'

'But none of it was intentional!' protested Mrs Wylde. 'She was led astray.'

'Led astray!' exclaimed the earl, his brows soaring. 'My dear Letty, we are talking of a young woman of twenty-three – twenty-four next month – not of a raw schoolgirl. Granted, Malcolm Brenner is a handsome fellow with some address, but a woman in Miss Chayter's position knows that she should be on her guard. Or has she not told you that I had to dismiss her for immoral behaviour?'

'I have every faith in Flora,' responded Mrs Wylde, taking hold of her protégé's hand, which at the moment seemed somewhat cold and unresponsive. 'She has told me of what occurred, and I believe her to be more sinned against than sinning. Furthermore I say again, I fail to see why my choice of travelling companion should in any way concern you.'

'Oh do you? I suppose the fact that she has once proved to be immoral and untrustworthy should not count with me. The reputation and good conduct of this party is in my hands. How can I possibly be easy in my mind if there is the chance that one of my party might be misbehaving with any man we chance to meet?'

'Oh hush, Leigh!' begged Mrs Wylde, looking again at Flora's set white face. 'Have some tact.'

'Why should I?' retorted the earl, glaring at Flora. 'Had she had a grain of tact and sensitivity, she would not have inflicted herself upon my party in this brass-faced way.'

It was at this point that Flora roused herself from the spell which seemed to have been cast upon her by the violent altercation which had taken place in front of her and about her, but in which she had never once been addressed by either party.

'You need not concern yourself, My Lord,' she said in a hard little voice. 'I would not dream of inflicting my immoral person upon your party. I shall return to England by the first available boat.' Pulling her hand away from that of Mrs Wylde, she ran out of the room and up the stairs, not even stopping to shut the door behind her.

Chapter Six

Mrs Wylde walked over to the door and closed it, then turned back to the earl.

'Oh Leigh, what have you done?' she exclaimed exasperatedly, her apprehension quite forgotten in her concern for Flora. 'I had only just managed to persuade her to come downstairs!'

'Persuade her? Why on earth should she need persuading?' asked Craythorne.

'Because she did not want to have to face you, of course. She knew it would be embarrassing for you both, she said. You don't seem to be very embarrassed though, Leigh.'

The earl flushed a little. 'I do not see why I should be embarrassed because I seek to protect the morals of my family,' he said. 'But as for persuading her, I repeat, I do not see why she should need to be persuaded. She has shown herself to be a young woman of considerable effrontery, in that knowing that she was to be of my party, she came anyway, regardless of the consequences.' It was Mrs Wylde's turn to flush and look away.

'Not exactly. . . .' she murmured. The earl stared at her. At once there came into his mind the memory of Flora's face on board ship when she had first encountered him. Her eyes had sparkled, her blonde hair had been whipping about her face, and altogether she had looked the picture of health and happiness, until it had dawned upon her who he was, and then an expression of shock had robbed her face of all its pleasure.

'God almighty!' he exclaimed. 'I wondered why you insisted that Matthew pick you up! All that nonsense about Peter's not having seen him for so long, and wanting to know how he was getting on was pure invention, wasn't it? You actually persuaded that young woman to come with you and gave her absolutely no indication that I was to be of the party, didn't you?'

'She had no idea of your presence at all until she saw you on the ship at Calais,' admitted Mrs Wylde, unaware that Flora and the earl had met earlier on during the voyage. 'She only realized that we were to be in the same party when M Dessin said a little while ago how pleased he was to be entertaining you. Well, if he is, you must be a lot more civil to him than you have just been to Flora, that's all I can say. Well, you will just have to apologize.' There was a long silence.

'Apologize?' said the earl dangerously.

'Yes, of course. How else will I persuade her to stay?' He said nothing, so she went on urgently, 'Leigh, you have done her an injustice, and the time will come when you will be forced to acknowledge it. I have known Flora from her childhood, and believe me, she is not what you suppose her to be. And besides, I have no abigail, no other woman with me. I cannot proceed without her.'

'Damn,' said Craythorne. 'And the problem is worse than you know.'

'Worse, how could it be worse, pray?' His Lordship looked a little shame-faced.

'Well – I have brought Catherine with me.'

'Catherine? Your niece? But she is only thirteen! What possessed you to bring her? I suppose you will say that that is all Flora's fault as well!'

'And so it is, in a way,' he replied defensively. 'Catherine was very much attached to Miss Chayter and when she left, the child showed signs of withdrawing in the way that she used to do. With the household arrangements in total disarray, Maria took to her bed – as always – and refused to take any action at all except to reach for her sal volatile. My trip had already been arranged, and I could neither let you down nor put off my own business. I therefore decided it would be better for Catherine to come with me than to be left there with no proper provision made for her. I thought that the journey would take her out of herself. She has been taking a great interest in the Continent recently. . . .'

'Under Flora's guidance,' put in Mrs Wylde. 'She really has told me everything, you know.'

'I have never disputed her ability to teach,' replied Craythorne. 'It is her other . . . propensities that worry me.'

'If only I could make you understand that Flora has no *propensities*, as you call them!' exclaimed Mrs Wylde, throwing up her hands in exasperation. 'Leigh, I beg you, if you have ever made an error of judgement in someone's character, then remember it now and give Flora another chance.'

The earl turned away and looked down into the fire. His companion had the feeling that his thoughts were far away. When at last he turned back, his face looked rather bleak, and he said, 'I have indeed made such an error, but my fault was in being rather too trusting on that occasion, so that particular example is not really to your advantage. However, I take your point and indeed I shall have to accede to your request out of sheer necessity.' Mrs Wylde clasped her hands together and smiled with relief, but he held up his hand. 'Listen, Letty, it has to be on two conditions: the first is that her behaviour must be exemplary. Let her make the tiniest slip and I shall have her escorted back to England, no matter where we may be. The other is that she helps to take charge of Catherine.' Mrs Wylde crossed the room and laid her hand on his arm.

'For the first, I can tell you now that there will be no problems. For the second, I am sure that she will want to help. She was very fond of Catherine, and suffered quite as much as Catherine when she left, you know. But how is it that you need help? Is there no one with you to care for her?'

'There was,' replied the earl shortly.

'Oh Leigh, don't tell me you have dismissed her, too!' exclaimed Mrs Wylde.

'No, I have not,' retorted Craythorne, nettled. 'Good heavens, anyone would think that I dismissed people all the time! For your information, Miss Chayter is the first person I have had cause to dismiss in several years, and I found it damnably hard to do. Catherine did have an abigail who came on board the ship with us, but she was never happy about sailing or coming abroad and after we had set sail, I found a note from the wench. Among other things, she had a sweetheart whom she did not wish to leave for so long, and she jumped ship just before we sailed. So you see, I am in desperate need.'

'Yes, I do see,' she replied, nodding sympathetically. 'The question is, will Flora be prepared to help you after the things you have said to her?'

After leaving the saloon, Flora had run upstairs in order to gain the sanctuary of her room. She had a vague notion that M Dessin addressed her on her way up, but what his words might have been she had no idea. Her head was too full of the earl's harsh voice and all the cruel things that he had said.

'How could he say such things about me! How could he!' she exclaimed, and for a brief time her anger buoyed her up. Soon, however, there came into her mind the memory of how the earl had surprised her in Malcolm Brenner's arms. Of course he had every right to think such things. How could he think any other? He did not really know her and could not be expected to realize that that was the greatest intimacy that she had ever permitted to his young kinsman. A tiny voice inside insisted that he should have allowed her to explain; and yet, in all justice, she had to admit that no explanation, other than an actual engagement, would have been acceptable. Besides, she had gone over all this ground before, many wearying times. Of far more pressing concern was her immediate situation.

How could she have been so foolish as to fail to realize that Lord Craythorne was to lead their expedition? With hindsight, it was clear to her that there were many things that had taken place and been said that should have given her a hint, but she had overlooked them, partly, she now admitted to herself, because she had not wanted to believe what they were telling her. She had been so excited at the idea of travelling abroad at last, and for the very first time – something she had thought she would never do – that she had closed her mind to anything that might prevent her going. Now she was paying the price for her wilful obtuseness. She would have to return to England after just a tiny taste of the adventure she had hoped to enjoy. It was too bad that after a new life had seemed to be opening up for her, one error appeared to be dogging her footsteps.

She found that tears were running down her cheeks, for she had started to cry without realizing it. She went over to the bowl on the washstand and splashed her face with water, then dried it with a length of linen which had been left for the purpose. She was just laying it down when the door opened softly and Mrs Wylde came in tentatively as if unsure of her welcome.

'Ah, there you are my dear,' she said, before Flora had time to say anything. 'I have brought a visitor to see you.' For one dreadful moment, Flora thought that it might be Craythorne, and she straightened her spine accordingly. She was astonished when a small figure emerged from behind Mrs Wylde and hurled itself at her.

'Miss Chayter, oh Miss Chayter!' exclaimed the newcomer, and Flora saw that it was Catherine.

'Catherine, my dear!' she cried, truly delighted at seeing her former charge. 'But how comes this about? Why are you here?'

'My uncle has brought me on a Grand Tour,' said Catherine. 'After you left, Mama went to bed and refused to get up again, and Craythorne said that it would be best for me to come away with him and leave her to absolute peace and quiet. Miss Chayter, why did you go? Craythorne won't tell me. Was it because of me? I wasn't naughty, was I?'

'Oh no, Catherine,' said Flora, hastening to reassure her. 'It was nothing like that.' She paused, uncertain as to how to go on, and Mrs Wylde stepped in.

'She left because I needed her,' she said. 'I wanted to go to Venice to visit my daughter and I needed her to be my companion.'

'Why did you not tell me?' asked Catherine. 'I would have understood.'

Again Mrs Wylde answered. 'She knew how much you wanted to travel and did not want to make you envious.'

'Well there was no need, because you see we are travelling too,' said Catherine. 'Only I do not know how we are to manage, because Florence ran away at the last minute and I have no one to look after me.' Suddenly her expression altered, and she caught hold of Flora's hand, her eyes shining. 'Oh Miss Chayter, could we all go together? Then you could look after me and tell me things. It would be so wonderful! Please say yes!'

'My dear, your uncle. . . .' she began.

'Leigh is agreeable to the idea,' put in Mrs Wylde. 'We only wait upon your consent,' she added, looking at Flora meaningly. Yet again, Flora had the most unpleasant sensation of having been manipulated. Unfortunately, she could not see how she could get out of this position, except by rejecting Catherine, who might quite reasonably believe that she had already been rejected by her once.

'Very well,' she said at last. 'If everyone else is in agreement, who am I to say no?' She was rewarded by Catherine with a hug and by Mrs Wylde with a grateful smile. Flora smiled back, but resolved to have words with her patroness later.

'Come along, then,' said the latter. 'M Dessin has already delayed dinner to suit our convenience. Let us go and eat, for I, for one, am starving.'

It was an ill-assorted party who met at the table, as far as moods were concerned. Lord Craythorne was courteous, but looked grim and unyielding. He accepted Catherine's news that Flora was to accompany them with a polite bow in Flora's direction and a murmured word of thanks, but he did not look as if her inclusion gave him any real pleasure. Mrs Wylde was still feeling guilty about her manipulation of Flora, and was consequently rather quiet. Flora herself said nothing during the meal. She sat down at the table, feeling sure that she would be able to eat nothing at all, but soon found that she was very hungry, and ignoring all the precepts that had been dinned into her about not eating too heartily and making pleasant conversation at the table, concentrated on her plate.

Catherine and Matthew Warren – whom Catherine addressed as 'cousin' – were the only ones in anything like a holiday mood, and even Mr Warren, who sensed his kinsman's disapproval but did not know its cause, was a little cautious.

The Hôtel d'Angleterre was famed for its hospitality and everyone finished the meal feeling that they had dined well; although some of their number would have been hard-pressed to remember what it was they had actually eaten. There was a moment when Flora thought that Craythorne was going to make a point of speaking to her, but she did not feel ready for any kind of confrontation that evening, and as it was Catherine's bed-time, she took her up to her room. Having helped her with her bed-time preparations, she then went to her own room and stayed there.

Once she had sat down, she became aware of what a long,

wearying day it had been, full of stresses and strains of all kinds. She began to prepare for bed, and was brushing her hair when Mrs Wylde came in.

'Flora, I am afraid I have put you in a very difficult position,' she said tentatively.

'Again,' added Flora, still brushing.

'Yes, again,' agreed the other with a sigh. 'I'm sorry, I really didn't mean to.' Flora laid down her brush and turned to look at her.

'I would like to know then, what you expected to be the result when you manipulated me into a position where I would be forced to accept Lord Craythorne's patronage,' she said forthrightly. 'You'll forgive me, ma'am, if I say that I find your remarks naïve in the extreme.' Mrs Wylde was silent, so after a moment or two, Flora went on, 'What did you think would be the result when you ushered Catherine in here? You knew how pleased she would be to see me! You have made it quite impossible for me to withdraw without hurting her, but then I suppose that was your purpose all the time.'

'Oh no indeed!' exclaimed Mrs Wylde, horrified. 'Such a thought was never in my head. Please believe me that I thought only to cheer you up.' After a short pause she added, 'I do not think that I could possibly have managed this matter worse. I am very sorry.'

Flora looked at her and reminded herself for what seemed like the hundredth time that this was the one person to whom she had turned in need, and who had not failed her.

'Forgive me if I was harsh,' she said, getting up from her chair, and coming over to the other woman. 'It is just that I still cannot see what purpose it will serve to thrust me into Lord Craythorne's company in this way.' Mrs Wylde put her handkerchief away.

'It is true that I did not expect us to have to have quite so much to do with him, for I did not know that Catherine would be here,' she said. 'But this could be even better. He will be able to see at first hand how well you teach her, and you are bound to spend time with her, whilst he escorts me. I shall be very surprised if his opinion of you has not changed completely by the time our trip is over.'

Despite herself, Flora could not help but smile at her optimism. Together, they helped one another to get ready for bed, and once the candles were blown out, they were both soon fast asleep.

Lord Craythorne had made it very plain that he wanted to make an early start in the morning, so the whole party were awoken at 7 a.m. Flora and Mrs Wylde – who had by this time begged Flora to call her simply 'Letty' – helped one another to dress, and Flora then hurried to help Catherine.

'It seems to me,' said Letty, 'that we must all three of us help one another. After all, you came originally as my companion. It is not fair that you should have to act as governess and nursemaid as well.'

'Catherine is very capable,' replied Flora. 'She is probably very nearly dressed already.'

'Even so,' said Mrs Wylde, 'I still want to be sure that you are not overburdened. I wonder whether we all ought to share a room in future? Or perhaps you could share with Catherine, and I could look after myself?'

Flora went to Catherine's room and found that as she had predicted, the girl was nearly ready. As they left the room, Catherine volunteered to go and see if she could help Mrs Wylde, and Flora carried on down the stairs. She heard some chatter coming from the kitchen area and for an instant was surprised to find that it was in French. She smiled to herself and walked into the dining-room only to find that Lord Craythorne was its sole occupant.

'I beg your pardon,' she said and made as if to withdraw.

'Please do not allow my presence to drive you away,' he said courteously but coldly. 'You are surely as much entitled to be in this room as I am.'

Flora made a small curtsy but said, 'Hardly, My Lord. You are the head of this party, whereas I am simply an employee.'

'Yes,' agreed the earl rather sourly. 'And my employee again it would appear, however little either of us may wish it.'

'Rest assured, My Lord, that you cannot possibly wish it any less than I,' flashed Flora, with a fire that surprised him. 'In any case, it is Mrs Wylde who is employing me, and not you. Whatever I may do to oblige you by way of taking charge of Catherine, I do because I have a regard for her.'

'And not for me, being your implication,' he replied, drawing his brows together. 'What exactly do you mean by that?'

Flora's colour rose a little, but she looked at him squarely and replied, 'I hardly know you, sir. It is impossible to have regard for a stranger – or to have any right to judge them.'

'I see. So you would maintain that I had no right to dismiss you on the grounds that I did not know you, is that it?'

'No, sir. You had a perfect right to dismiss me and to disapprove of what I did, for I know that it was wrong. But you have no right to use that one incident as a basis upon which to judge everything that I do.' He looked at her in silence for a moment, with an expression which held something of respect.

'You have a fine line in argument,' he said eventually. 'You are right, of course, Miss Chayter, but in matters concerning the welfare of my niece I cannot afford to take chances. One error was enough, I'm afraid.'

'And yet you have been prepared to allow me another chance,' murmured Flora.

'Only because I have been compelled to do so, believe me, Miss Chayter,' he replied, coming closer to her. Flora felt a slight inward shudder. 'I assure you, ma'am, one slip-up and I will personally drag you back to Calais and put you on the first boat to Dover.'

Fortunately, before there was an opportunity to say more, the door opened to admit Catherine and Mrs Wylde, and almost immediately afterwards, Mr Warren, and the conversation turned to the day's travelling.

'Which way will we be going, Craythorne?' asked Catherine. 'How far do you think we shall go today?'

'We shall have a look at the map after breakfast,' the earl promised, his tone softening as he spoke to his niece. Sure enough, as soon as the meal was over, they returned to the parlour where His Lordship got out his map, rolled between two sticks for convenience. 'Show me where Calais is,' he said. Catherine looked down and found it without any hesitation. 'Good,' he said. 'Now find Paris for me.'

Flora stood near the door. She loved maps and would dearly have loved to examine this one, but the earl was standing very close to it, and at present she felt that she would rather have been in the room with a poisonous snake. It was only when Catherine turned and said, 'Miss Chayter, do come and look,' that she drew closer. The earl politely made room for her – or, as she mentally told herself, drew back the skirts of his riding coat so that they would not be contaminated by her person. 'There it is,' said Catherine, pointing to Paris.

'And how far is it from Calais to Paris?' asked Craythorne.

'A little under two hundred miles,' replied Catherine. 'Which route shall we take?'

Flora had been studying the map with interest and had reached her own conclusions about this, so she put out her hand to indicate the post road through Boulogne. The earl was similarly prepared to do the same, so they reached out at the same time and their hands touched. Flora drew back immediately, blushing, and the earl also quickly moved his hand, but indicated to Flora with a gesture that she might continue.

'From Boulogne, I imagine that we shall go through Montreuil and Amiens. After that, I expect, Chantilly and Saint-Denis.'

'Exactly so,' agreed Craythorne. 'So as we have a long way to go, I suggest that we prepare to leave immediately.'

It took several days to accomplish the journey to Paris. As predicted, the earl did choose to ride, but not all the time, and there were long periods when he and Flora were obliged to occupy the same small space. At such times, the presence of Catherine was an undoubted blessing. Unaware of the difficult relationship existing between her favourite male relative and her former governess, she chattered quite naturally with one then the other. Flora had not seen the earl in conversation with his niece before, and she was impressed with the way that he listened thoughtfully to her questions, and answered them without patronizing her. Flora found herself forced to acknowledge his undoubted intelligence, and she wished that she herself could converse with him without constraint.

As they entered the inn when their day's travelling was done, Mrs Wylde apologized for the way in which Flora had been thrust into the earl's company. Her concern was obviously so genuine, that Flora told her not to think anything more about it.

'Had we but given the matter any serious thought, we would surely have anticipated the situation,' she went on. 'After all, you cannot expect the poor man to ride halfway across France, however much he may like the exercise, just to avoid my presence.'

Without their realizing it, the earl had entered close behind them and he now said blandly, 'Sympathy from you, Miss Chayter? I should never have supposed it!' before passing them in the corridor and going to speak to the hotelier.

M Corbieux had already done his best to puff up His Lordship's consequence; and the ladies very much hoped that this would result in comfortable rooms and aired beds. This particular inn was respectable enough, but offered very little by way of accommodation. Flora, Catherine and Mrs Wylde were obliged to share one room, and the earl, Mr Warren and M Corbieux another. When Mrs Wylde ventured to protest to M Corbieux, he replied by assuring her that she should be grateful that the whole party did not have to share one room.

'Oh good heavens, no!' exclaimed Flora, her hands flying to her cheeks when she was told.

'That is just what I said,' answered Mrs Wylde eagerly. 'But M Corbieux said that sometimes there are such brigands about that we would be grateful to have the gentlemen in with us! I was thankful that Catherine was not listening, I can tell you.'

'I should think so indeed,' agreed Flora. 'Brigands! Does he think it likely that we shall encounter any?'

'I do not think so,' replied Letty, shaking her head. 'After all, we are a sizeable party; and for all that you and Leigh are at odds, I can tell you that there are few men upon whom I would depend more to disperse a company of brigands.' Flora recalled how like a pirate the earl himself had looked when they had arrived at Calais, and she found herself bound to agree.

They made a brief stop at Amiens in order to view the cathedral, which they all acknowledged to be very fine. Whilst there, they took time to walk a little, and admire views of the river Somme. During the next part of the journey, whilst Lord Craythorne was with them in the coach, Catherine looked out of the window and exclaimed, 'Those are strange looking plants! What are they? Are they trees?'

It was not plain to whom she was speaking, and so both the earl and Flora replied, as with one voice, 'Those are vines.' Craythorne made a gesture with his hand, as if to invite her to continue, but Flora shook her head.

'No, please go on, My Lord,' she said. 'I am sure you know

far more about wine than I do.' Suddenly aware of how this might sound, she coloured, and the earl raised one eyebrow.

'It would be a little strange if I did not, Miss Chayter,' he replied. It was the most pleasant exchange that they had had so far during the journey.

They also spent some time at Chantilly and went to have a look at the Prince de Conde's palace there. It was certainly worth a visit, having agreeable walks with views of canals, fountains, and cascades, and constant glimpses of ornamental birds, their colourful wings enhanced when viewed through the spray in some of the water gardens. Catherine enjoyed feeding the fish by hand, and Matthew took a great interest in the stables, which were magnificent, if rather dirty. There was similar evidence of neglect in other parts of the palace, for the planetarium was in a poor state of repair. The earl looked at it with his brows drawn together in that expression of disapproval which for once, Flora was relieved to see, was not directed at her.

'Shameful,' he murmured as he looked around. 'Shameful.' Flora was thinking the very same thing, and briefly their eyes met in a moment of complete accord. She found herself hoping that this might be the beginning of a better relationship.

Sadly, the good understanding between them was destroyed very soon, and not through any fault of Flora's. It happened that Mrs Wylde was very anxious to purchase some of the lace for which Chantilly was very justly famed as an extra bride gift for Jane. Unfortunately their walk in the palace gardens took longer than they expected and they found themselves without the time to purchase the fine work that she had admired on their way to take their walk that morning.

'Oh dear,' murmured Mrs Wylde. 'I would so much have liked some. Well, it cannot be helped. We cannot afford to delay in the morning. Leigh is so business-like, and cannot tolerate any kind of dallying about.'

'I could slip out before we set off tomorrow, if you like,' suggested Flora. 'If you will attend to Catherine, I can soon have my packing done, and we will cause no delay.'

After breakfast the next day, Mrs Wylde gave Flora the money necessary for the purchase, and the younger woman hurried to the shop. The elderly shop-keeper had only just arrived and was busy unlocking the premises, which activity seemed to Flora to take an interminable amount of time. She held her peace, nevertheless, not wanting to give an unfavourable view of the English nation to this courteous old man. By the time the weather, the prince's gardens and Flora's journey had been discussed and half the lace in the shop had been politely rejected in favour of the piece that Mrs Wylde had chosen in the first place, more time had passed than Flora would have supposed possible. She hurried back to the inn to discover the horses already put to, and everyone ready to go. The earl was standing in the inn yard dressed for riding, his feet astride, and he was slapping his whip impatiently against the side of his boot. His brows were drawn together in the familiar black bar that Flora had come to dread.

'At last,' he said tersely. 'Do you realize how long you have kept us waiting?'

'Indeed, I am very sorry,' began Flora, 'but—'

'Not sorry enough to prevent you delaying us all, it seems,' he retorted. 'Allow me to point out, Miss Chayter, that the purpose of this party is not to provide you with shopping expeditions.'

'But indeed, My Lord—'

'Oh, enough!' he snapped. 'Be silent and get into the coach. We have been held up quite enough by your lack of consideration.' Abandoning any further attempts to explain herself, Flora hurried to the coach to discover Mrs Wylde on the point of getting out.

'My dear, I must put this right,' she said concernedly. 'I told Mr Warren that you had gone on an errand for me, but he cannot have passed the message on to Leigh. I must tell him immediately.'

'Oh no, Letty, pray do not!' cried Flora, not sure whether she was more angry at the injustice of the earl's accusation, or mortified at being the unwitting cause of the delay. 'Let us get on our journey. There will be time enough for explanations later.'

Letty agreed, although unwillingly, and seemed to be very ready to discuss the quick temper and unreasonable impatience of the earl, but Flora, mindful of Catherine's presence, threw her a warning glance and suggested a word game instead.

They stopped briefly at an inn for lunch but there was no privacy and no opportunity for private conversation. Lord Craythorne was coldly courteous to Flora when absolutely necessary, but otherwise ignored her, giving most of his attention to Catherine.

That evening saw their arrival in Paris. They were to stay at the home of a friend of Lord Craythorne, the Comte de Saint Croix, in the Rue Saint-Honore. Flora was convinced that she would be described as some kind of inferior and undesirable servant, and consigned to sleep in the attic. The earl, however, merely introduced her as 'the friend of Madame Wylde' – and rather implied by his tone 'no friend of mine' – and thereafter paid her no further attention.

The *comte* seemed an unlikely friend for the earl to have. He was taller than Craythorne, with features more finely drawn, and a laughing eye, and a pronounced air of fashionable elegance. Much to Flora's surprise, however, the earl seemed to unbend in his friend's company, and to become much more relaxed. Naturally, the responsibility of caring for his party had been of great concern to him. It must be very pleasant for him not to have to think about the safety and well-being of those in his care, Flora decided. His thick brows separated themselves from one another, his mouth turned up more at the corners, and he was even heard to laugh on several occasions. Flora looked at him with interest. It was amazing the difference that happiness made to his usually severe countenance.

The *comte* showed great interest in each of his guests, asking Mrs Wylde if this was her first journey to the Continent, and if she was enjoying herself.

'Oh yes indeed,' she replied, determined to find the opportunity to correct an earlier misunderstanding. 'I came once before, but neglected to bring back any mementoes of my travels. This time, I am making sure that I buy a little something everywhere I go.'

'An excellent idea,' replied the *comte*, with enthusiasm. 'Have you found anything of interest yet?'

'Certainly,' she answered, glancing at Flora. 'I bought a length of lace in Chantilly – although that is for my daughter and not for myself.'

'A fine choice,' said the *comte*. 'They make the best lace in the world at Chantilly, would you not say so, Craythorne?'

'I am no expert,' replied the earl. 'I believe that that is the accepted opinion. Certainly two of the ladies of my party were enough swayed by it to spend their money.' He did not look at Flora, but his tone became noticeably colder.

'Ah, so Miss Chayter, you were tempted also?' asked the *comte* smiling.

'No, His Lordship is mistaken,' she answered, colouring a little. 'I only purchased lace for Mrs Wylde this morning at her request.' She and the earl looked at one another, and this time it was his turn to colour.

Aware of some tension in the atmosphere, but not knowing its cause, the *comte* with his fine social sense, sought to dispel it by turning to Catherine and saying, 'And what are your most lasting impressions of the journey so far?'

When dinner was over, the ladies withdrew and once they had reached the saloon, Catherine wandered over to the harpsichord.

'At least now he knows,' said Mrs Wylde, *sotto voce.*

'As if that will make any difference,' returned Flora in the same quiet tone. 'His opinion of me is so low that it has already sunk without trace. I cannot suppose that this discovery will make the slightest difference to him.'

It was not very long before the gentlemen joined them. Catherine was just finishing a piece as they entered, and she made as if to leave the instrument.

'Oh do not say we are too late!' exclaimed the *comte.* 'That harpsichord has not been played since my mother died. I should not have allowed Craythorne to persuade me to keep drinking brandy with him if I thought that the penalty would be quite so severe!'

'Persuade!' exclaimed the earl with mock incredulity. 'I am but a guest here. I was not the one doing the persuading! But do play for us just once, Catherine; then I think it must surely be time for you to retire.'

The earl had decided that as Catherine was undertaking a very grown-up expedition, she should be allowed to dine with the adult party for the duration of the tour. Truth to tell, she was feeling a little tired now, but obediently she sat down again, and began to play a piece by Clementi. She was a competent pianist and played with considerable accuracy. Her performance was not a gifted one, but she played with modesty and seriousness, and at the conclusion of her piece there was warm applause.

'Now bed for you,' said the earl with a smile when she had finished.

'I will take you up,' said Flora getting to her feet.

'By no means,' exclaimed the *comte.* 'Cosette shall take Miss Brenner upstairs whilst you remain with us.' He walked across the room to ring the bell. As he was doing so, Lord Craythorne caught Flora's eye, and began to walk towards her. She wondered whether he was going to apologize for misjudging her, but as he drew near, his brows unfurrowed by that intimidating frown, the *comte* turned back towards them, saying with a twinkle in his eye, 'Bad enough that we should lose one beauty; it would be a wicked sin to deprive us of two. Do you not agree, Craythorne?'

'As you say,' replied Craythorne, his expression becoming colder, and he turned away to speak to his cousin and Mrs Wylde who were looking at a book of sketches of Italy which the *comte* had brought from his library. Flora was surprised to find herself feeling disappointed. The *comte* chuckled playfully.

'Aha! I see what it is! I am treading on his toes as they say, and he is just a little jealous, I think.' Flora's expression turned from one of confusion to absolute horror as he was speaking.

'Oh no,' she protested. I assure you, *Comte*. . . .'

'*Mademoiselle*, I hesitate to contradict a lady, but I know what I know,' he replied with great satisfaction. 'What say you we really give him something to think about?'

Chapter Seven

They spent a week staying with the Comte de Saint-Croix, and it was a week during which Flora experienced very mixed feelings. The *comte* could not be swayed from his view that Lord Craythorne was personally interested in her, and consequently took every possible opportunity of flirting with her under the earl's nose. To begin with, Matthew Warren took his cue from the Frenchman and, for a time, there was between them a relationship of friendly rivalry for her attentions which appeared to amuse them both very greatly, and Lord Craythorne not at all, for the earl, after a contemptuous glance or two, largely ignored her, although she was conscious from time to time of his scornful gaze. Flora could not deny that up to a point it was pleasant to have two personable gentlemen paying her attention, but she wished that the *comte* in particular would not be quite so fulsome. She could not help thinking that Craythorne, had he wished it, could easily have moderated the attentions that she was receiving at very little trouble to himself, but he showed no signs of doing such a thing. She wished that he could have been more sensitive to her feelings.

The sensitivity that he appeared to lack was eventually shown by his cousin. They went as a party to visit The Louvre and admire the pictures. Saint-Croix had excused himself as he had another appointment to keep. After they had entered the building, the party split into two, Craythorne walking with Catherine and Letty, and Mr Warren taking his place at Flora's side. Without Saint-Croix to set the pace, Matthew abandoned his flirtatiousness, and talked with so much interest and lively humour that Flora found herself in complete charity with him. So much more comfortable was she that she felt emboldened to say, 'What an agreeable, friendly morning this is.'

'Just so,' he answered, looking sideways at her. 'All that flirting – you don't really like it above half, do you?'

'If you only knew,' she answered with a sigh.

'Well, I won't do it any more, if you don't like it.' They walked on to look at another picture, unaware of the earl's gaze upon them. 'I don't know about the *comte*, though,' he went on doubtfully. 'He seems to look upon it as a kind of sport.'

'Yes, he does,' agreed Flora. She hesitated for a moment, not sure whether to go on. 'The worst of it is, he has somehow got the idea that Lord Craythorne is . . . is interested in me, and he thinks to make him jealous.'

'Leigh! Good heavens!' exclaimed Mr Warren with a whoop of laughter which abruptly stopped as he turned and saw his cousin quite close to them. 'Excuse me,' he murmured, with an expression of comical dismay, and went to speak to Catherine and Letty. Craythorne took a step or two closer to her, and it took all her resolution not to shrink back.

'Up to your old tricks, madam?' he purred, his voice full of menace.

'My Lord?' she murmured, her hand at her throat. She did not grasp his meaning, and could not think in what way she had offended him.

'Don't play the prude with me,' he snapped. 'Understand this, Miss Chayter. Matthew is dear to me as Malcolm has never been. Do anything to hurt him and I will destroy you.' He turned to follow the others, but it was a minute or two before she felt she had sufficiently recovered from the shock of his words and his tone in order to do the same.

After this, Craythorne's attitude seemed to change subtly. He appeared to give more time and attention to his cousin, whilst at the same time encouraging the young man to look around him independently of the party if he so wished. Matthew no longer flirted with Flora, but the *comte*'s interest did not wane, and Craythorne watched the whole proceedings with a cynical eye.

Flora tried very hard not to let the situation spoil her enjoyment of the adventure, but it was not easy. Matthew was of an open, confiding disposition, and whilst no longer inclined to flirt, he was still ready to offer his friendship. Flora was not romantically drawn to him at all, but she liked him, and they were very much of an age. Clearly, however, the earl looked upon any kind of relationship between them as something to be discouraged for fear that his young kinsman would be corrupted by the temptress that he obviously believed her to be. She could not help but regret that a man who was clearly intelligent and well read should fail so spectacularly in his judgement of her character, and that that failure should mean that she was deprived of a friendship that she was sure she would have enjoyed.

Paris itself she could not help but view with a degree of ambivalence. On the one hand it was one of the dirtiest places she had seen. It seemed to be quite impossible to escape from the smell of human filth, and she began to realize that the *comte*'s carrying of a scented handkerchief, which he raised periodically to his nostrils, was not an affectation, but a vital ingredient for comfort. On one occasion, when they were out, she even had to steer Catherine away from the sight of a respectably dressed man relieving himself in the street.

On the other hand, it was perfectly true what every traveller said – the buildings were absolutely magnificent. The gloomy splendour of Notre-Dame was particularly impressive. Catherine took her sketchbook with her when they visited it, and Flora would have liked to have given her full attention to the work that she was producing, and to her reactions, but unfortunately, everything was coloured by the presence of M le Comte, who had very different ideas of how best to spend the time. He was not so insensitive as to ignore Catherine's efforts, but he soon began to hint that a tête-à-tête in the gloomy cloisters would be more to his taste. Lord Craythorne was talking to Mrs Wylde nearby, but also ostensibly observing what Catherine was doing. Flora felt certain that his real purpose was to see whether she would put a foot wrong.

'Come now, *mademoiselle*,' said the *comte*, his blue eyes twinkling. 'I know this cathedral well, and there is much I wish to show you.'

'I do not doubt it, *m'sieur*,' she replied pleasantly. 'However, I do feel that my place is with Catherine.'

'Catherine is surrounded by admirers,' he responded. 'Indeed, I suspect that there are almost too many of us for her to concentrate. We can return shortly to observe her progress.' To refuse now would almost seem churlish, but Flora made one more attempt.

'Indeed, *m'sieur* . . .' she murmured, looking at Lord Craythorne, and hoping against hope that he might come to her assistance. He returned her look with a cold stare.

'You do not object to Miss Chayter's enjoying herself, *mon ami*?' put in the Frenchman.

'I doubt that any objection of mine would affect Miss Chayter's enjoyment,' replied the earl. 'In any case, she is never happier than when she is enjoying the attentions of men; the more, the merrier.'

'*Chut*!' exclaimed the *comte* as they walked away, shaking his hand as if burned. His face showed such a comical parody of dismay that Flora could not help smiling, despite her irritation.

'We certainly touched a nerve there, I think.'

If Flora hoped that the *comte* would back off a little after this incident, then she was to find herself mistaken. If anything, he became even more flirtatious, whilst the earl looked on in an even more cynical manner, as if everything that happened merely confirmed his opinion of her. She did not even have so many opportunities to confide in Mrs Wylde as before, because they were naturally given separate rooms in the *comte*'s spacious home, and during the daylight hours, the company were usually together. Flora did not dare try to seek out Mrs Wylde at night, for fear of what construction the *comte* might place upon finding her wandering the corridors of his house in her night attire.

One of the last excursions that they went on during their stay was a visit to the palace of Versailles. All the ladies looked forward to this with keen anticipation. Even Lord Craythorne appeared to be more mellow, despite the fact that Saint-Croix had insisted that he purchase a new suit of blue velvet, and have his hair thoroughly powdered.

'No no, *mon brave*! You simply cannot go anywhere dressed as you are!' exclaimed the *comte* with comical dismay, when the earl ventured to suggest that he had enough clothes already. 'People will think that you are a wild man!'

Flora and Mrs Wylde also purchased new gowns for themselves and for Catherine. Flora had demurred, but Mrs Wylde had insisted.

'Certainly you must have a new gown,' she declared. 'You have seen how elaborately the Parisiennes are dressed. And after all, you must allow me to make some recompense to you for the uncomfortable situation in which you have been placed. I do not know what ails Leigh these days, I'm sure. He's as grumpy as a bear with a sore head.'

Reluctantly Flora agreed to the proposed purchase and she was glad that she had done so when she saw the sophisticated appearance of the other ladies at Versailles. She would have felt under-dressed indeed in her usual plain blue travelling dress.

Versailles itself proved to be something of a disappointment to them. Large it might have been, but the ladies found it dark and rather dirty, and inside, many rooms were rather poky. The whole place resembled a labyrinth in which only the *galerie des glaces* seemed to possess any grandeur or majesty. Catherine, however, was very struck by it as it was her first visit to a real royal palace, so Flora and Mrs Wylde held their peace as much for her sake as in order not to say anything that might be overheard and taken amiss by anyone with influence. When Catherine realized that the king was actually present, her eyes grew as round as saucers.

'May we meet him?' she asked Saint-Croix.

'I think not today,' replied the *comte.* A moment later one of the royal attendants came over to the *comte* and whispered in his ear. 'It seems I am summoned,' he said ruefully. 'No doubt to explain why it is so long since I have been here. If I am not back in five minutes, then I suggest you go into the gardens as we agreed before and I will find you there.' He turned away from them, then on impulse suddenly turned back. 'Stay though,' he murmured, his eyes sparkling. 'The king may be more likely to release me if I am accompanied.' To Flora's surprise and dismay, he seized hold of her hand. 'Come, you shall be my protection,' he said. Flora could think of no excuse. Craythorne said nothing and she dared not look at him. To engage in a dispute in such a public place would be absurd and unmannerly, so she went with the *comte,* dragging to the front of her mind everything that she could remember about the correct procedure to be observed when meeting royalty. There was no time for her to feel nervous.

Evidently, her curtsy and her manner were satisfactory, for the king seemed pleased with her, complimenting her on her beauty, and on her command of the French language. Sadly for Saint-Croix, however, the king indicated that he still wished for some private conversation, so the *comte* escorted her back to the party.

'I will join you as soon as may be,' he assured them, before returning to his king.

'Come, let us go into the gardens,' said the earl, adding under his breath, 'I for one have had quite enough of this tomfoolery.'

The room, though cold, was rather stuffy and the air was none too fresh, so the ladies were glad to repair to the garden, and even Catherine had now looked her fill at the king and was ready for some fresh air.

The gardens, like the palace, were huge and magnificent, but not particularly beautiful, and Flora did not feel regretful that they had left their sketch books behind. Mrs Wylde, Mr Warren and Catherine wandered ahead to look at one of the fountains, leaving Flora and Craythorne to walk together. Flora was preparing herself to face his anger, so she was rather taken aback when he remarked blandly, 'Rather a satisfactory day for you.'

'I beg your pardon?' asked Flora.

'Let me advise you not to read too much into it, however,' he went on as if she had not spoken. 'Royalty can be notoriously fickle and Saint-Croix does have some royal blood in his veins. Sadly, the demands of the king have to take precedence over your amours, I'm afraid. I trust you don't expect me to flirt with you instead. If you do, you'll be sadly disappointed. I'm not very attracted by soiled goods.'

Flora was so surprised that she could only stare at him. It was not his words that shocked her so much as the bitterness of tone, which had increased as his speech had continued. With his Parisian clothes and his powdered hair he had appeared to have put on a new urbanity, so much so that she had almost begun to relax, but his determination to think the worst of her was clearly undiminished. As she said nothing, he continued with considerably less cordiality.

'I think I warned you that I would have no hesitation in escorting you to Calais if you put a foot wrong, and believe me, I am very sorely tempted to do so.'

'My Lord, you are being grossly unfair!' exclaimed Flora indignantly.

'Am I indeed, ma'am? So I suppose that you have not been flirting with Saint-Croix to the point of indecency almost from the very moment of your arrival?' They had stopped walking and were now standing facing each other next to the fountain that their three companions had just been inspecting before walking on.

'No I have not,' declared Flora indignantly. 'It is he who has been flirting with me.'

'Whilst you were all unwilling, I suppose,' answered the earl sarcastically. Flora flushed a little.

'No, I was not unwilling, but. . . .'

'Of course not; as no doubt any man might discover.' Flora's hand flew up to strike him, but he was too quick for her and seized her by the wrist in a vice-like grip. 'The truth hurts, does it? No, madam, you'll not slap me. I've already saved my family from one scandal of your making. Don't for a moment think that I'll allow you to stir up another. And you can abandon any plans you may have for seducing my cousin. I'd sooner be seduced by you myself!' There was a moment's utter stillness during which a current of some kind of feeling flashed between them; then Craythorne's grip on her arm slackened and she tore herself free.

'I would rather suffer the worst torments of Hell,' she declared. 'I thought I loved Malcolm Brenner, and believed that he loved me in return. And for your information, My Lord, I have never even thought about seducing Mr Warren, whom I must say seems to be singularly unfortunate in at least one of his relations!'

'You are impertinent,' he replied, his brows drawn together. 'May I remind you, madam, that it is not my conduct that is in question, but yours; and in particular your unbridled flirting with a man far higher in station than Brenner. There was never the slightest chance of Malcolm Brenner's marrying someone in your impecunious circumstances. If you think that just because Saint-Croix introduced you to the king he would seriously look your way then I have to tell you that you are mistaken. As a mistress perhaps—'

Automatically, Flora lashed out at him again, and this time her hand did make contact with his cheek, with a crack of sound that shocked them both. They stood looking at each other for a few moments; it was Flora who found her voice first.

'How dare you?' she cried, her face flushing almost as red as the angry mark that had appeared on Craythorne's face. 'When you are the one who brought us here in the first place! The *comte* is your friend, and far above me in degree, as you say. What do you think I should have done in the palace just now, with everyone looking on? Shake him off and say "No, I don't want to meet the king, thank you very much?" '

'Whilst we have been in Paris, he has hardly left me alone! How was I supposed to get rid of him without being rude? Do you really suppose that I wanted to have him hanging over my shoulder all the time when there was a whole city to be seen and experienced? There were so many questions to ask, and so much to talk about! Do you think it likely that I wanted to discuss the colour of my eyes or my gown?'

'Miss Chayter . . .' began the earl, but Flora barely allowed him to speak.

'One word from you, My Lord, and he would have left me alone!' she said, a sob catching in her throat. 'Just one would have been enough. Am I so utterly unworthy of your protection?' With that, she swung round and gathering her skirts, fairly ran towards where the other three were standing beside one of the canals, her pace as rapid and undignified as that sedate place had seen for quite some time. On her arrival amongst them, she was pressed by Mrs Wylde to sit down, whilst Matthew looked at her a little anxiously.

'I thought my cousin was escorting you,' he said, looking round.

Fearful that he might guess they had had a disagreement and perhaps surmise part of the cause of it, she said quickly, 'Yes, but I think he caught sight of the *comte* and did not want to lose him in the gardens. Have you seen anything worthy of your sketchbook, Catherine?'

'Yes, Miss Chayter,' replied Catherine. 'I was wondering whether I might draw the king when I get back to Paris, and if I would remember his appearance well enough. I tried hard to look carefully without staring. How lucky you were to meet him in person. What did he say to you?'

'Very little indeed,' replied Flora, anxious to make light of the whole incident. 'I am sure we will all do our best to help you.' Looking up, she was relieved to see the earl and the *comte* approaching, and thus bearing out what she had said to Matthew Warren.

'M de Saint-Croix will surely be able to help,' said Mrs Wylde, 'for he had a long private conversation with the king.' She explained to the *comte* what was required, and the Frenchman threw up his hands in an entirely Gallic gesture.

'Ah, *madame*, but to remember what he wore! Does a man ever really notice another man's clothes? Were it a beautiful woman, now . . .' and allowing his voice to tail off caressingly, he turned to Flora half-bowing, his eyes sparkling.

'Enough, Robert,' said the earl good-humouredly. 'Miss Chayter is far too tired to listen to your nonsense, and far too intelligent to believe a word of it. Indeed, I think we are all quite tired, and Catherine is looking a little pale. What say you all to leaving now and finding a hostelry where we can slake our thirst?'

The whole party being in agreement, they left Versailles with very few regrets. They found an *auberge*, 'Le Coq d'Or', quite close to the palace and there they refreshed themselves. Some lemonade was found for Catherine and the adults shared a bottle of wine, together with a plate of sweet cakes. It was a great relief to be able to sit down and relax after having been on their feet, and on their best behaviour too.

On the surface, Flora managed to maintain an unruffled demeanour, but inside, her mind was in turmoil. She tried to recall exactly what she had said to the earl, and how rude she had been, but all that she could remember with any clarity was the loud report that had been brought about by her slapping him across the face. What would be his opinion of her now, she wondered. It would hardly be surprising if he personally supervised her packing, frog-marched her back to Calais, and flung her without ceremony on to the very next out-going vessel. She drank the wine that was put in front of her and obediently sampled the cakes, but she would have had difficulty recalling the flavour of either, or even the colour of the wine.

That night they were to dine quietly at home as they were to leave Paris the following morning. They had a long day of travelling ahead of them, so Catherine was to eat in the room that had been designated as the nursery whilst they were staying with the *comte*, and then retire early. After she had changed for dinner, Flora went to make sure that her charge was happily settled, and fortunately, this was soon established. A young woman called Cosette had been appointed as nursery maid for as long as their visit lasted. She was a cheerful, petite, quick-witted girl with dark hair and snapping bright eyes, and Catherine had taken a great fancy to her. Cosette was the senior of the two by only six years, and they seemed to chatter happily together, despite the fact that Cosette only had a smattering of English. Catherine was a little shy of speaking in Saint-Croix's company, but found herself able to practise her French quite comfortably with Cosette and her accent was noticeably improving.

It took Flora only a moment or so to realize that she was not needed in the nursery, and, consequently, she found herself going downstairs for dinner in good time. She entered the drawing-room to discover Lord Craythorne waiting there already. Clad in black with a white waistcoat, with his hair once more free of powder and tumbling about his shoulders, he looked much more himself, and somehow more formidable.

Flora had been doing little other than brood over her dismissal, which now seemed to be more and more likely to her with every passing hour. Her visit to Catherine had, for a time, succeeded in turning her mind to other things. The events of the day had come back to her afresh as she descended the stairs, and the memory of the way in which she had struck the earl became so powerful that she almost expected to find him sporting a black eye. When she came face to face with him in the drawing-room she whitened a little, but stood her ground and looked at his apparently unmarked face anxiously. The earl rubbed his cheek significantly.

'Looking for the scars, Miss Chayter?' he asked, in a tone that she found impossible to analyze. As she could not think of a response to this, she said nothing, and silence fell between them for a short time. As it did not appear that she was about to be dismissed quite immediately, Flora ventured to say at last, 'I am pleased that Catherine has taken so well to Cosette. It has encouraged her to be more confident with her French.'

'That I had noticed,' replied the earl. 'In fact, I have decided to include Cosette in my party. Saint-Croix is agreeable, and she can come back to his household after the tour is over.'

Flora felt her heart sink. So she was to be sent home after all. Craythorne had managed to secure a replacement for her. No doubt he would be able to talk Mrs Wylde round also. 'I see,' she said in low tones.

'You don't approve?' he questioned. 'I felt sure you would. No doubt she will also be able to give you and Letty some assistance on the journey.' Flora looked up, a puzzled expression on her face.

'Give me assistance? You are not dismissing me then?'

'Again?' he murmured, a wry smile on his face. Flora continued to look at him steadily. It was so long since she had seen him look at her with any other expression than anger or contempt. A feeling of warmth began to creep over her.

'But I . . I struck you,' she whispered.

'You did indeed, and a handsome blow it was. Is that to be included in your instruction of Catherine? I agree that a gentleman should be made aware that his remarks are not to a lady's taste, but there are less violent methods, surely?'

Flora had to smile at this; but having done so, she turned away, saying, 'I tried less violent methods, but you did not listen.'

'No, I didn't, and for that I ask your pardon.' Flora turned back towards him, her eyes full of surprise. He paused for a moment, then went on, 'Whatever may be my opinion of the way in which you conducted yourself at my sister's house, you are presently a lady travelling under my protection, and I failed to make that clear to Saint-Croix. Consequently, I exposed you to rather more gallantry than was acceptable, then blamed you for it. For that I also ask your pardon.'

Flora flushed. 'You suggested . . . you implied. . . .'

Craythorne also flushed a little, and interrupted her. 'That also was unacceptable. Dear me, I seem to be apologizing for rather a lot, don't I?'

Suddenly remembering that he was in some senses her

employer, Flora looked down and murmured, 'You are very good.'

'To go back to Malcolm Brenner,' went on the earl. 'You are not the first young woman that he has pursued in a household which he has been visiting. A governess is in a peculiar position, neither protected by the fellowship of the servants' hall, nor entitled to the support of a member of the family. You should not have succumbed to his blandishments, Miss Chayter, that I still maintain. But I should have taken more account of your vulnerability.' The kindness of his tone was not something that she had come to expect from him and for some absurd reason it made her want to cry.

'Thank you, My Lord,' she managed. 'You are—'

'If you say I'm very good again I shan't be answerable for the consequences,' he replied ironically. 'I'm not very good; neither am I very bad; but I think I did you less than justice.'

At that moment, the door opened to admit Mrs Wylde, escorted by Saint-Croix. Mr Warren appeared seconds later and very soon after that, dinner was announced. They had been very well served by the *comte*'s chef during their stay. This evening, he put forth his best efforts, and surpassed himself. Flora had not realized how Craythorne's attitude to her had affected her appreciation even of the food in front of her. Now, with his disapproval lifted, she found herself enjoying this meal more than any she had eaten since the start of the adventure.

The conversation was very much concerned with the itinerary which they were to follow. There was more than one way of travelling to Lyons, and Lord Craythorne had decided to go by road, rather than by water.

'The river journey can be very pretty as I recall,' put in Saint-Croix. 'I last went down the Saône some five years ago and found it very agreeable and quite exciting.'

'Perhaps,' agreed Craythorne. 'But pray recall that I will have four females to consider, and I understand that the company on the boat can be a little mixed.'

'Then on all accounts it is to be avoided,' declared Mrs Wylde. 'Catherine cannot be exposed to that.'

'Am I alone in thinking, Letty, that your reluctance has more to do with avoiding another boat journey than with protecting Catherine from undesirables?' quizzed the earl. Everyone laughed.

'I must confess that that was also a motive of mine,' admitted Mrs Wylde. 'However since you have already decided on the land route, Leigh, my difficulties with travel by water are not worth discussing.'

'So where will our route take us?' asked Matthew Warren. He was dressed this evening in pale-blue satin, with his dark curly hair neatly confined with a ribbon and carefully powdered. Paris life seemed to be bringing out the dandy in him, Flora reflected.

'Through Briare and Pouilly, then two or three other towns before you reach Lyons,' answered Saint-Croix, elegant as ever in his powder and paint, and dressed in apricot satin with a white waistcoat embroidered with silver. 'Briare, I think, has a tolerable inn, but after that, be prepared! You have Corbieux with you and he seems to know his business, so rely on him. Ah, how I wish I were coming with you! But engagements do not permit it.'

Flora breathed a sigh of relief. She was far too thankful for the new mellowness in Craythorne's attitude to risk jeopardizing it now.

Chapter Eight

They bade farewell to their genial host the following morning and were soon on their way, their party now including Cosette who rode in the coach with them. Both the earl and his cousin were riding. Should they both wish to ride inside at once, it would now make everyone a little squashed, but Mr Warren seemed to enjoy the view of the countryside that he obtained from riding on the box, and indeed both gentlemen enjoyed taking a turn to drive now and then. The weather continued fine, so consequently they spent very little time inside the coach.

'After Lyons, I understand that the journey will become more mountainous,' remarked Mrs Wylde, 'and we may have some snow. Probably the gentlemen will want to travel inside then, and we shall not mind being a little crowded – in fact, it will keep us warmer.' Flora could not help finding the prospect of snuggling up to Lord Craythorne for warmth a little unnerving, but she held her peace.

The inn at Briare turned out to be the best of those that they visited on their journey to Lyons. After that the accommodation proved to be somewhat less than perfect. Mrs Wylde put things rather less politely.

'Indeed, Leigh, we appear to have returned to the Dark Ages!' exclaimed Mrs Wylde. 'Could you not have found us somewhere more salubrious?' Lord Craythorne held out his arms in a disclaiming gesture.

'Acquit me of any responsibility here, my dear Letty,' he said. 'Take the matter up with M Corbieux if you have any complaints; the itinerary was arranged with his advice.'

Mrs Wylde did as her childhood friend suggested, but later reported to Flora in the room that all four females were to share that she had gained no satisfaction in that quarter.

'He has told me that this is the best inn to be found for miles around,' she complained. 'At least the landlord is honest, if you please!'

'It does not look too bad,' murmured Flora, looking round at their room. 'At least there are enough beds for all of us.

Mrs Wylde sniffed. 'If you can call them beds,' she said disdainfully. 'And who can tell who may have slept in them last? Remember that scoundrel we saw upon the road going the other way? What if he were the last one to sleep in them?'

'I doubt if he slept in them all,' answered Flora with a smile. 'Anyway, Cosette will put our own sheets on for us, and it will be just like sleeping in our own beds.'

Cosette, although only having been with them for a day or two, had already proved to be invaluable. She had cheerfully kept Catherine entertained, teaching her rhymes and stories in French and making up games to amuse her, thus allowing Flora and Mrs Wylde to talk, join in, be silent, or even doze according to their present fancy. She was also ready to help by fastening buttons, tying laces and bows and dressing hair. Even now, she was bustling around, stripping the beds, muttering in French about the filthiness of provincial inns, and getting out their own sheets to spread them on the mattresses.

'Our own beds!' exclaimed Mrs Wylde scornfully. 'My mattresses do not have lumps like that!'

Catherine, pressed into service by Cosette, said, 'Look,

ma'am, I am managing to smooth some of these lumps out. You can have this bed with Miss Chayter, and Cosette and I will have the other.'

Mrs Wylde glanced towards the second bed, which certainly looked inferior to the one that Cosette and Catherine were making, and her gaze softened.

'You're a good child,' she said, 'and I'm a thoughtless wretch to be complaining like this! I am sure that all the work you and Cosette have done will make the beds very comfortable; and after all, it is only for one night.'

Flora, smiling at her patroness's efforts to appear more cheerful, decided to help with the beds before starting to prepare for dinner. She picked up the sheets and walking across to the second bed, she drew back the covers, then uttered a piercing scream. There on the bed was a mouse.

Mrs Wylde, catching sight of the mouse, screamed too, whereas Cosette, with business-like efficiency, seized the large, chipped bowl which stood on the rickety cupboard and advanced upon the luckless rodent, whilst Catherine looked on with interest.

The mouse, clearly feeling that a quick disappearance was called for, scurried in Flora's direction, and Flora leaped back towards the door, which flew open to admit Lord Craythorne, who sprang across the threshold. He had obviously been in the middle of changing, for although he was wearing the same breeches that he had worn during the day, he was in his stockinged feet, having taken off his boots, and had stripped to the waist. His Lordship crouched like a cat, his sword in one hand, the other stretched out for balance. His dark eyes flashed and the wild black mane tumbling about his shoulders was echoed by the luxuriant black thatch on his chest. Flora almost collided with him as she retreated, and he grasped her arm and thrust her firmly behind him, whilst he swiftly scanned the room.

Catherine and Cosette, who had not been much disturbed to start with, were the first to speak.

'It's all right, Craythorne,' said Catherine. 'Cosette has caught him.'

'Cosette?' murmured the earl, the light dying out of his eyes as he straightened a little. He looked round the room again, glanced at the only cupboard of any size, and then looked back questioningly at Cosette.

'Be calm, *m'sieur,*' said the Frenchwoman, one hand on the bowl which was now resting upside down on the bed. 'I 'ave 'im in 'ere.'

'In there?' echoed the earl faintly, allowing his sword arm to drop.

'*Mais oui*! It is only – 'ow you say – a smile!'

Everyone looked at her in puzzled silence until at last Catherine said, 'No, Cosette; not *sourir*; *souris*. A mouse, not a smile.'

Craythorne burst out laughing. 'You mean that I have hurried here to your defence, just to vanquish a mouse?' he said ironically. 'Who screamed?'

'I am afraid it was I,' confessed Flora, blushing. 'I am not normally afraid of mice, but it took me by surprise. I found it in the bed, you see.'

'Yes, I can see that that would be something of a shock,' replied the earl, turning towards her. Suddenly Flora felt rather hot and her heart seemed to skip a beat.

'It was very gallant of you, Leigh,' smiled Mrs Wylde. 'Particularly as you are *en deshabille.*' Suddenly the earl seemed to become conscious of his state of undress, and he flushed.

'If you will just allow me to trespass a little longer, I will remove the offending rodent for you,' he said.

'I will take your sword Craythorne,' said Catherine. 'Only please do not kill the little mouse. He was as frightened as we were.'

The earl heaved a sigh, then taking up a plate from a table near the fireplace, he slid it under the bowl, picked up the whole and carried it to the door. Cosette, who had snatched up a poker, snorted with disbelief at the sentimentality of the English, as Catherine followed her uncle down the passage, sword in hand, in order to make sure that he kept his word concerning the mouse.

'Come, Flora,' said Mrs Wylde, business-like now that the mouse had gone. 'Let us check that mattress for holes. I don't want to risk finding any more mice in here.' Flora, who had by now recovered her equilibrium, hurried to help her, glad of any activity which might serve to banish from her mind the memory of his lordship's stalwart, semi-clad figure.

The food provided by the inn at dinner was plain but reasonably wholesome, and the wine was excellent, so the inn was felt to be not so bad as it might have been, despite the mouse. During the meal, the earl came in for a little gentle teasing, to which he responded in very good part.

'I very much regret that I was talking downstairs with Corbieux,' said his cousin. 'Otherwise I would have joined you in vanquishing such a fearsome foe.'

'But you would then have spoiled Leigh's moment of glory,' replied Mrs Wylde. 'Thanks to his courage, we shall all put him on a pedestal from now on.'

'Not Cosette,' answered the earl. 'I believe she was quite contemptuous of our actions in saving the mouse.'

'Yes, she was,' put in Flora. 'She muttered for quite five minutes after you had gone, and prowled about the room, poker in hand. I believe that she was rather disappointed at not finding any more, and even now, she may not have put the poker away.'

'In that case, I had better not make any more sudden entrances,' he said, smiling. Briefly, their eyes met, before Flora looked down again at her plate.

'What a good thing you decided to employ her,' said Matthew to his cousin. 'She is clearly a remarkable young woman. Do we know anything of her history?'

'She is the daughter of one of the tenant farmers on an estate belonging to the *comte*,' replied Flora. 'She was in Paris not as a servant, strictly speaking, but in order to visit her aunt, who is the *comte*'s housekeeper.' All this she had learned during the day's travelling, whilst Catherine and Mrs Wylde had been enjoying a doze. She did not add that Cosette's father had sent her away in order to discourage an attachment between his daughter and a young man whom he felt to be rather undesirable.

'Do you not mind?' Flora had asked her, mindful of her own feelings when she had been parted from Malcolm. Cosette had shrugged.

'There are always other men,' she had said with a grin.

'Her countrywoman's background would account for her fearlessness with the mouse,' Lord Craythorne remarked in response to Flora's words at the table.

'Like Flora's, you mean,' said Matthew with a grin. He and Flora had progressed to first-name terms after a word game that they had been trying to teach to Cosette that day during one of Matthew's brief rides in the carriage.

'Miss Chayter, I am sure, shows her courage in other ways,' answered the earl. Flora looked at him, and quickly looked away again.

That night in bed, after Cosette and Catherine had gone to sleep, Mrs Wylde whispered to Flora, 'You know, my dear, that incident with the mouse has given me confidence.'

'In what way?' Flora whispered back at her.

'Well, you saw how quickly Leigh came through to defend us. You know why he came, don't you?'

'Well, he heard me scream.'

'He thought we were being attacked,' insisted Mrs Wylde. 'I

will never forget how dangerous he looked, ready to defend us from who knows what peril.'

'He was certainly – very prompt,' ventured Flora.

'Prompt indeed,' murmured her companion with a yawn. 'Not even stopping to dress! We will certainly be very safe with him around! Well, goodnight, my dear.'

'Goodnight,' replied Flora automatically, wishing that her bedfellow had not brought Lord Craythorne's gallantry and state of undress to the front of her mind. Since their argument at Versailles, and his apology afterwards, his greater courtesy towards her and his responsible consideration of the whole party had caused her to change her opinion of him. She had noticed that disreputable characters took one look at His Lordship's powerful figure and steered a wide berth around their party.

He was clearly delighted to be upon the Continent, and that vitality of his which was always there under the surface, was very much in evidence. Flora was beginning to find herself thinking about him more than she felt was wise.

She thought back to the night when Lord Craythorne had appeared and discovered her with Malcolm Brenner. How would things have fallen out if the two men in the scene had been exchanged to play one another's part? One thing was certain, the earl would never have left her to face alone the consequences of what they had done, had he been the man she was meeting. Into her mind came the moment during that last meeting when she had been clasped in Malcolm's arms, having received his kiss. In her mind's eye, as she looked into the young man's face, it was transformed into that of Lord Craythorne!

Flora gave a horrified gasp, turned over and quickly recited all the speeches from Shakespeare that she could remember until at last she fell asleep.

Chapter Nine

After the vicissitudes of country taverns and dubious accommodation, the travellers were very thankful to reach Lyons, where they could be sure of a good inn. They stayed for two nights at the Dauphin, and were very pleased with the way in which they were treated. The *patron* was anxious that everything should be to *milor*'s satisfaction, and made sure that the very best rooms were at their disposal.

Among other things, the linen on the beds was clean and well aired, and Cosette took the opportunity to get their own sheets laundered ready for the next part of the journey. She clearly had a talent for housekeeping, perhaps inherited from her aunt, M le Comte's housekeeper, and she was now thoroughly enjoying the opportunity of ensuring the comfort of the party. M Corbieux clearly regarded her with approval, but Flora could not help noticing that Cosette had another admirer. Matthew had been very struck by Cosette's resourcefulness in dealing with the mouse, and he was obviously intrigued by the attractive Frenchwoman.

Flora was enjoying the journey much more, now that the earl had ceased to regard her with scorn. She had not realized how much difference it would make to her comfort when he fully accepted her as a member of his company. Previously, it had been as if the cloak of his protection was cast about the party, with herself just allowed to cling on to the edge of it by dint of her connection with Mrs Wylde and Catherine. Now that she was fully included, the difference was subtle, but unmistakable. There was no longer any familiarity from other guests, or slowness of service from servants. One look at His Lordship's powerful figure and keen glance, and would-be philanderers kept well away.

They still looked, though, for Flora was well worth a second glance. Always a pretty girl, the excitement and interest of travel gave her features animation, and more than one gallant would have attempted to set up a flirtation with her had they not encountered the earl's forbidding expression. On one occasion in particular, Flora was glad of his presence. She had mislaid a handkerchief and thinking that she had dropped it downstairs, she went to look for it, only to find that a dark, slender Frenchman had picked it up and was looking at it. It happened to be one of a pair that Jane had embroidered for her birthday one year, so she was particularly anxious to get it back.

'Excuse me, *m'sieur*, but I believe you have my handkerchief,' she said politely.

'Indeed,' he replied, smiling and waving it in his hand. 'Doubtless *mamselle* would like it returned to her?'

'Certainly I would, if you please,' answered Flora.

'One wonders why just a handkerchief should be so important,' he mused, showing no signs of returning it.

'It was given to me by a friend,' said Flora beginning to feel annoyed and a little uneasy. 'Please give it back to me.'

'But of course!' he exclaimed. 'The only question is, what penalty would be appropriate for its return?' Flora hesitated, unsure of what to say. While she was still silent, the earl, who had come in unnoticed, spoke from behind her in pleasant tones, but with an unmistakable air of authority.

'*Mam'selle* has said "please", which is surely the only penalty any gentleman should require.' The young Frenchman straightened a little, and immediately returned the handkerchief with a bow.

'But of course,' he said. 'I was about to give the handkerchief to *mam'selle.*' He paused for a moment, then added impishly, '*M'sieur* can surely not blame me for seeking to further my acquaintance with so lovely a young lady.' Craythorne's expression remained courteous, but he gave the Frenchman no answering smile.

'I will inform *mam'selle*'s aunt of your approval,' he said drily. 'But we must not keep you from your business, *m'sieur.*' He held the door open politely.

After the Frenchman had gone, Flora turned to the earl and said, 'Thank you, My Lord. You are doubtless thinking me foolish to care so much about a handkerchief, but it was one that Jane had given to me.'

'Not at all,' he answered, his expression more relaxed now that the French gallant had gone. 'I can think of no reason why you should not be entitled to reclaim your own property.'

'What a nuisance it must be for you to have to care for all of us,' she continued. 'It would have been so much simpler for you to have travelled across France on your own.'

'Simpler perhaps, but not nearly so eventful!' he returned with a smile. 'When the whole trip was planned, I knew that I would have responsibility for those in my party. I just forgot what an added complication it can be when one of the group is young and pretty.'

That day happened to be the one when they were to leave Lyons, and Flora had much to think about, but in her mind, one phrase kept returning to her like a litany: he thinks me pretty!

After Lyons, the next town of any size was Chambery. At this point, they had already begun to climb and, ahead of them, they could see the mountains that lay between them and Italy. Flora had visited Wales once some ten years ago, and she had read much about the whole region that they were to visit, but no amount of reading, and no remembered visit from childhood could have prepared her for the awesome majesty of the scenery in front of her. Mrs Wylde was silenced for once; Catherine voiced the thought that was in all their minds.

'Craythorne, are we really going to climb that mountain?' They were standing in front of the inn at which they were to stay. It was situated at the far end of the town, and so they had an excellent view of the road ahead of them, as it wound steadily upwards, and eventually disappeared from their field of vision.

'Certainly,' he replied. 'But don't be anxious! We shall have plenty of help.'

'And we can all help each other, can't we?' answered Catherine. For no accountable reason that Flora could think of, her eyes met those of Lord Craythorne, before they both looked quickly away.

That evening, before they retired, Catherine said to her uncle, 'How will the carriage manage to get us over the mountains?'

'This is where we leave the carriage behind,' he replied. 'It will be kept in store until we return. We will hire another after we have crossed the mountains. Those travelling in their own carriages sometimes have them dismantled and carried by mule, but I felt that that was hardly necessary with a hired conveyance.'

'So how will we get across the mountains?' persisted Catherine. 'Will we have to walk?' The earl chuckled at the outraged expression on the face of Mrs Wylde.

'Can you see how entranced Letty is at the very idea?' he said. 'No, Catherine, we will be carried on chairs by porters.'

'You do not say so, Leigh!' exclaimed Mrs Wylde, her face still a picture of horror. 'Heaven send that they are surefooted!'

Thankfully, the following morning her prayer was answered favourably. The porters who were to have charge of them were sturdy, capable-looking men with a good knowledge of the terrain. By the time their belongings had been loaded on to mules, and they themselves had been taken up in chairs by porters, with additional men walking alongside to take a turn in carrying, their party was a sizeable one indeed. Their number was depleted by one, however, for it was here that they said goodbye to M Corbieux, whom they had got to know so well. He seemed sorry to part from them all, and particularly Cosette, who did not seem nearly so affected by the separation, but the handsome *pourboire* that Lord Craythorne pressed into his hand softened the blow.

The day was a bright and sunny one, but they were soon glad of the beaver hats and gloves and bear-skins in which they had been swathed, for it became colder as they climbed, and drew within reach of the snow. Somewhat to her surprise, Flora found that she was to travel in the chair at the front of the party. Letty flatly refused to do so, having, she said, no desire to see the treacherous terrain before she actually had to cross it. Flora was rather nervous to start with, for the men carrying her seemed to leap so rapidly from one rock to another that she was sure that any minute she would be deposited at best into a snow drift, and at worst down one of the ravines that plunged to one side or the other of them from time to time. But as the journey proceeded she lost her fears, and made the most of her opportunity to observe the landscape. Never had she longed more fervently for skill with an artist's pencil and brush!

To start with, Lord Craythorne and his cousin chose to walk. Catherine demanded her uncle's company, but Matthew hurried ahead and walked with Flora. Although he was much the same age as Flora herself, he seemed to her to be more like a boy in his eagerness to leap from rock to rock, and show that he was as agile as the porters.

'Have you heard Letty?' he asked her. 'I never knew anyone to squeal so much. I just hope she won't start an avalanche!' Flora laughed but looked round a little nervously all the same. For all its magnificence, the scenery was certainly alien and at times forbidding.

She was very glad when, during a brief halt on a plateau, Craythorne came up to Matthew and said in rather repressive tones, 'I think it is time that you and I took to our chairs.'

'But why? This is excellent sport,' protested Matthew.

'Neither of us is as nimble as these fellows. You may think you're a mountain goat, but I can assure you that you're not; and I have no desire to have to break the news to your mother that you are lying at the bottom of a foreign precipice. I'm sure you will find plenty of other opportunities to impress Miss Chayter.' So saying, he turned on his heel and walked towards the chair that was awaiting him.

'But I . . .' began Matthew. Then he stopped and turned to look anxiously, not at Flora, but at Cosette. Quickly, the Frenchwoman said, '*Milor*' is right, *m'sieur*. No good can be served if you break your neck.' Whereupon he took his place in the chair provided for him without further protest. Flora glanced at Cosette, but she was looking away, and there was no opportunity for further conversation.

Crossing the mountains took them four days altogether, and such was the cold at that altitude that they were thoroughly thankful to find any lodging at night that would provide them with beds and warmth. It spoke much for their situation that they were even glad to take refuge in the little inn at Lansleburg which was certainly the most primitive accommodation that any of them had come across, offering as it did only one room for the whole party to sleep in. Unfortunately, they were obliged to stay there for an extra night, because of a sudden descent of mist which did not disperse until it was too late for them to travel on. Under those circumstances, it was clearly absurd to stand on ceremony, and the whole of the group gathered together after the meal to tell tall stories until it was time for bed.

Cosette was completely undisturbed by her grand company, and with great aplomb, related a story purporting to be a true one concerning a remarkable cow which once resided on her father's farm. This amazing beast yielded ten gallons of milk a day, until the time when the dairymaid forgot to thank her; whereupon she disappeared without trace the following day, never to be seen again. Catherine's eyes grew as round as saucers.

Matthew applauded enthusiastically, exclaiming, 'Splendid, splendid!' and then relapsed into blushful silence.

'Now you, Craythorne!' cried Catherine. 'Please!'

'I'm not sure that I have anything remarkable to recount,' he replied. 'So I will content myself with merely telling you the story of a journey that I made on horseback, from Edinburgh to London. I was due to meet someone on a matter of business so I was not able to delay my journey, otherwise I should certainly have done so, for as I called for my horse to be saddled, it was pouring with rain. I remember quite clearly that it was on a Wednesday morning that I set out. As I left the city, however, the storm slackened considerably, and there appeared the brightest and most distinct rainbow that I have ever seen. I was just admiring it, when something happened in the light, perhaps a more penetrating shaft of sunlight than any other. Suddenly, I found myself standing, as it were, in the light at the end of the rainbow, and the scenery about me seemed to be bathed in a myriad of colour. I hardly wanted to move away, but I knew that I did not have time to linger. The rainbow appeared to follow me for a short time, but then I rode on and left it behind.

'I will not burden you with the details of my journey – where I stopped, or for how long I stayed – suffice it to say that although the incident remained at the back of my mind, I was not always thinking of it. But there were occasions when it would come back to me. Riding through a forest, the light would seem to be more violet than golden, or waking in the morning, a shaft of sunlight would fall on my face that was green rather than yellow.

'Eventually, I arrived in London, and according to my calculations, I had got there exactly on the day that I had expected. I retired for the night, slept well, and woke the following morning. As I drew the curtains in my room, the sunlight that streamed in was pure gold. I prepared myself to go to my lawyer's office in Chancery Lane, but when I got there, I found to my surprise that I was not expected. "My Lord, you need not have cut short your visit in Scotland", he said. "I was not expecting you for another six days". To my amazement, I had arrived in London on the same day that I had set out from Edinburgh. Not a single day had passed.' A murmur of applause greeted this story.

'Oh, Craythorne,' exclaimed Catherine, 'do you think there really is magic at the end of a rainbow?'

'That I cannot say,' he replied. 'But one thing is certain: my lawyer will tell you that I was indeed several days early for my appointment with him after my journey from Edinburgh.'

When it was time for them to repair to the chamber that they were all to share, the ladies took one end of the room and the gentlemen the other. The ladies retired first, with Cosette and Catherine sharing one bed, and Mrs Wylde and Flora sharing the other as before. Mr Warren and Lord Craythorne retired to the bed allotted to them after the ladies had had time to settle into their beds. By great good fortune, there were no other travellers needing to sleep there that night.

As she lay in bed listening to the gentlemen making their preparations for retiring, Flora, in that strange state that is not really wakefulness and not quite sleep either, reflected idly on the perversity of human nature which makes one long to open one's eyes, even though one knows one should keep them shut. There came into her mind the picture of Lord Craythorne, stripped to the waist. Had he undressed as far as that, or further? Flora came suddenly wide awake with shock at the indecency of her thoughts. She pressed her hands to her ears and closed her eyes tightly. She was not sure how long it took her to fall asleep that night.

Magnificent though the Alps were, they were all thankful to find themselves on the Italian side, and making their descent towards the plains of Piedmont. The scenery was magnificent, with cascades first on one side and then the other, and then gradually cultivated fields beginning to make their appearance. Sometimes up among the precipices and rocks a tiny village could be observed; Flora found herself wondering how anyone could ever manage to live in such a remote area. Further down, they began to catch a glimpse of little towns, with scattered church spires, and occasionally, they would hear the distant sound of church bells coming to them through the clear air.

The roads in this part of Italy were not good, and so it had been arranged that they were to continue by mule until they reached Turin, where they would meet their *vetturino*, the man who was to act as their guide and courier, drive their carriage and attend to the horses. They reached Turin on the second day after leaving the mountains, and were very pleased to find themselves settled in a commodious inn, in which there was enough accommodation for them all to have rooms of their own, including Cosette.

'Do let us stay here for a day or two,' begged Mrs Wylde that evening. 'I am heartily sick of being perched on that mule, and feel that I need a little time to recover.'

'By all means,' replied the earl genially. 'I understand that inns of this standard are the exception in this part of the world, so we might as well make the most of it. Furthermore, I have learned from another guest here that there is an acquaintance of mine now living in Turin; and I would very much like to renew an old friendship.'

'If we are to stay, then may we go and do some sketching?' asked Catherine of Flora.

'By all means,' replied Flora. 'Let us go tomorrow – if everyone else is agreeable?'

'I will escort you, if I may,' said Matthew eagerly.

'Naturally, you are free to go anywhere you please,' replied Craythorne shortly. 'And Letty may come with me to the Palazzo Condisi – if that will fit in with her plans,' he added with rather more cordiality. Mrs Wylde, delighted at the thought of going to a palazzo, readily agreed.

The following morning, however, they encountered a setback concerning their arrangements, for Catherine awoke with a sick headache, and was clearly unable to go anywhere.

'I will stay behind and look after her,' said Flora to Mrs Wylde in low tones outside Catherine's room.

'Nonsense,' replied that lady forthrightly. 'Cosette can very well do that. It is not as if she needs nursing care, after all. By the way, my dear, did you realize that Leigh's old acquaintance is a woman? I have to say that I am exceedingly curious to meet her! Apparently, it is someone he met in London a few years ago when her husband was alive, and over there on business. My dear, you may imagine how my mind is seething! Suppose she is an old flame of his? But I will tell you all about it later on.'

'Yes, do,' replied Flora; and if she wondered why her pleasure in her own expedition had seemed to diminish, she put it down to the fact that Catherine was unable to join her.

Turin was built in the form of a star, with a large stone at its centre, and by standing on the stone, a good view of the surrounding countryside could be gained. Before retiring on the day of their arrival, Flora had walked to the stone, which was only a short step away from their hotel. Her intention was to make up her mind about where to go in order to do her sketching by getting an over-view first. The route by which they had arrived was the most direct towards the mountains, but this was lined with a long avenue of trees, which would hardly make for an interesting subject. It did not take her long to decide upon the angle from which she would draw the Alps. The resulting sketch would make an excellent reminder of her adventure.

Matthew was still to act as her escort, but at the earl's insistence, they were to take with them the daughter of the innkeeper for the sake of propriety.

'For the Lord's sake don't be so stuffy,' Matthew protested to his cousin. 'I've known Flora for ever!'

'You have only known her since the beginning of this journey,' retorted his cousin crisply. 'Different standards and views of acquaintance obtain on the Continent. We should not want to cause gossip.'

'Definitely very stuffy!' muttered Matthew, but he agreed to the presence of Antonia all the same. For the short journey out of town, they borrowed a small open carriage from the inn, which was driven for them by one of the grooms employed there. The day was good for sketching, with a light breeze and fluffy clouds, all of which would add interest to the chosen subject. Once they had reached an ideal spot, Matthew helped Flora down, and the groom unhitched the horses and prepared to enjoy a much more restful day than would otherwise have been his lot. Antonia, a pleasant, rosy-cheeked girl, carried a basket which the innkeeper's wife had pressed upon them, and which Flora suspected contained wine and other refreshments for later. Matthew insisted on carrying the sketch pad, and once they had found a conveniently placed log, spread over it the rug which he had been carrying on his arm.

'May I sharpen your pencils for you?' he asked her.

'It is already done,' she replied with a smile, opening the tin in which she kept them. For a time, Matthew watched her work with courteous interest, but then, with a murmured apology which cited, among other things, the tiring nature of the previous day's journey, he lay down on the grass, propped himself up against the log and closed his eyes. Very soon, his gentle breathing told Flora that he was fast asleep. She glanced across at Antonia. The girl was sitting with her back against a tree, her eyes shut, the sewing that she had brought lying in her lap. Flora smiled to herself and turned back to her sketching, but within a few moments, her pencil grew idle in her hand. On impulse, she put on one side the sketch of the scene before her, and began instead to draw the sleeping man lying to one side of her. As she drew, she found herself wondering whether his formidable cousin would look as young and defenceless if sleeping thus.

He must indeed have been tired, for he did not wake until she was just finishing her picture.

'That's better,' he sighed, getting to his feet and stretching. 'Let's see how it's coming on.'

'I couldn't resist,' murmured Flora as he came over to her side. 'You're not often as still as that when I have my pencil in my hand!'

'I say, that's very good!' he exclaimed. 'I hadn't realized my likeness to Leigh was so marked, though. What a daunting thought!' Flora had looked up to see his reaction. Now, looking down at the picture, she realized that in fact she had drawn her version of how Lord Craythorne would look in a similar situation. She blushed with vexation, but Matthew did not see, for at that moment, Antonia had woken up, and he was beckoning her over to admire the drawing. Antonia exclaimed with admiration at Flora's skill, and gave her to understand that a sketch of herself to present to her betrothed, the son of another local inn-keeper, would be very much appreciated. Flora promised to do what she could, and pleased with this assurance, Antonia went to get out the refreshments.

'Nothing like fresh air to give you an appetite,' remarked Matthew, as he expertly opened the wine and poured her a glass. The inn-keeper's wife had packed bread, cheese and cakes as well as wine, and Flora, suddenly realizing that she too was a little peckish, put aside her sketching in order to enjoy what had been provided for them.

'Well, here's to absent friends,' said Matthew, raising his glass. Flora accepted what he had said without further thought, but he clearly took her silence to be a request for further clarification, and he added; 'Leigh, Letty, and Catherine, you know; and . . . and Cosette.'

'Ah,' murmured Flora, and she responded, 'absent friends.' Then, unable to resist the temptation of probing a little, she said craftily, 'I think I must have cause to drink Cosette's health most of all today, because had she not stayed behind with Catherine, I would have had to miss my day's sketching.'

'I wonder how Catherine is,' replied Matthew, not rising to the bait. Then adding, as if he could not help himself 'What a pity that Cosette has to stay in on such a fine day – I mean, that they both had to stay in.'

'Yes indeed,' agreed Flora. 'Perhaps when we get back, Catherine will be feeling sufficiently recovered for you to take her for a walk.'

'Yes, I could certainly do that,' he replied cheerfully. 'They would be glad of an airing, I dare say.' For some time now, Flora had been drawing her own conclusions about Matthew and Cosette, but she resolved to pry no further. Besides, in her experience Matthew, a sociable person, was very likely to tell her more if she would only be patient.

She was right. After their small repast, the remains of which Antonia cleared away, Flora went back to her original sketch.

Matthew, now fully refreshed after his nap and his lunch, watched the developing scene with interest.

'How I wish I had some kind of talent – like drawing, or music,' he said easily, giving the impression that if he did wish for such a thing, he did not wish it very deeply.

'You have a gift for managing your cousin's affairs,' answered Flora. 'That is probably much more useful.'

'My cousin is very good to me,' said Matthew, 'and very indulgent of my failings. You must surely have realized by now that it is far more the case that he manages mine, for he is much more efficient and astute than I am.'

'I have noticed that he is very business-like,' admitted Flora.

'He doesn't need a secretary at all,' confessed Matthew. 'It is only due to his generosity that I am employed, and that my mother is cared for; but I must not bore you with my family history.'

'I'm not bored, but I don't want to pry,' said Flora. Matthew needed no further encouragement.

'You see, Leigh's father and my mother were cousins. They spent a lot of time together, so Leigh grew up thinking of Mama as his aunt. When Mama came out, she fell in love with a soldier – my father – and eloped with him instead of dutifully marrying the man that my grandfather had picked out for her. She and my grandfather were never reconciled, and when he died, he had still not spoken to her. He never even saw me, his only grandchild, and left all that he possessed to a distant relative, leaving my mother penniless.'

'How dreadful!' exclaimed Flora, turning aside from her sketch to stare at him.

'I know my mother felt it,' replied Matthew. 'But even now, she never speaks against her father. My parents were very happy, though, whilst my father was alive, but when my father was killed in action, my mother found herself with no resources, and with me to care for. I was then a boy of ten.

'By that time, both Leigh's father and my grandfather were dead. It was Leigh who took us in. He was twenty-three.'

'And you have been living with him ever since?'

'Yes, Mama lives in the dower house at Craythorne as a kind of unofficial dowager, since Leigh's mother died when he was a schoolboy.' He paused briefly, then went on in low tones of unmistakable sincerity, 'I can never hope to repay his kindness to me – to my family. So I do the best for him that I can. The last thing that I ever want to do is to let him down or . . . disappoint him.'

'I am sure that he is very proud of you,' said Flora. 'It is clear that he holds you in considerable affection.'

'Yes, I know. I would like to take the whole responsibility of caring for us off his shoulders. Not that he ever throws our dependence upon him in my face, but. . . .'

'. . . But you want to provide for your mother yourself. It is very commendable that you should wish to do so.'

'Yes, but how? Leigh would like me to marry well. . . .' He broke off and turned away, then looked back at her and said, 'What do you do if the dictates of your heart go directly against everything that your head tells you you should do?'

Flora laid down her pencil. For a moment, she felt herself to be right back at Mrs Brenner's house, believing herself to be in love with Malcolm, and thinking that love would conquer all. How could she, who had made such a foolish mistake, possibly give advice on this subject?

'You have to be very sure of your own feelings – and of those of the other person,' she replied. 'And even then, it is not easy. Look at the difficulties experienced by your own parents.'

'But Leigh would never behave in the way that my grandfather behaved,' he said confidently. 'He has too generous a spirit.' Flora thought of the way in which the earl had caught her when she had fainted and procured breakfast for her on the very morning when he had dismissed her. She also thought of the reference he had written her, the large sum of money he had bestowed upon her, and his promise that he would help her should she have proved to be with child by Malcolm Brenner.

'He is generous,' she agreed thoughtfully.

'The thing is, I do not want to arouse his anger – and I fear that he will be angry – until I am completely sure of what I want to do. You will not tell him. . . ?'

'I do not think that I have anything to tell,' she replied.

'Flora, you are a good fellow!' he exclaimed, then added, I beg your pardon!'

'Not at all,' she answered, laughing. 'I always wanted to have a brother.'

She began to pack her things away, and as she was doing so, Matthew said diffidently, 'I don't suppose I could beg you for a small favour?'

'If it is in my power,' she said.

'It is just if I wanted to . . . to send a message, or see her . . . you see, we are so much thrust upon one another during this journey, and. . . .' Flora closed her tin of pencils and looked at him with troubled eyes. Briefly, she gave him an edited version of her romance with Malcolm and her dismissal at the earl's hands.

'So you see that having had such an experience myself, I will do nothing to endanger Cosette's reputation,' she concluded. It was the first time that the name had been spoken between them during this part of the conversation. 'I know how easily that can happen, and with what dire consequences.' Matthew coloured and looked her straight in the eye.

'I give you my word that I do not intend to besmirch her reputation, or spoil the happy comradeship that we all enjoy. As soon as I am sure that our feelings are unalterable, I will go to Leigh and tell him, I promise you. But I must see her alone. Will you help me?'

'I. . . .'

'It is not as if Leigh is my guardian, after all. Please, Flora?'

She sighed. 'If you give me your word that this will only be for a limited period, until you feel able to speak to your cousin, then I will help you. . . .' Matthew gave a whoop of delight.

'Thank you!' he exclaimed. 'You're a true friend. Do you think that this fine weather will hold for the rest of the day?'

'So that you can take Catherine for a walk?' asked Flora innocently as they walked back to the carriage. Matthew had the grace to blush.

'Such a splendid house, Flora,' said Mrs Wylde later on as they met before going in to dinner. 'Everything in the first style of elegance!'

'And the *contessa*?' asked Flora, because she felt she must. 'Was she very beautiful?'

'Oh, extremely so. And so affable! She was delighted to see Leigh – and he to see her, too; you could tell! I have not seen him smile and laugh so much for a long time!' She lowered her voice conspiratorially. 'Apparently, she is a wealthy woman in her own right and need answer to no one. Someone was telling me that she would like to marry again and return to her native England.'

'I did not realize that she was an Englishwoman!' exclaimed Flora.

'Oh, yes; and if she is looking for an English husband, well! But I must not say more. However, it did seem to me,' she went on, contradicting herself immediately, 'that she was enjoying Leigh's company in a most particular way! But you will see all this tomorrow.'

'Tomorrow?'

'Why yes! The whole party, that is Leigh, myself, yourself and Matthew are invited to dine at her house tomorrow. There is to be dancing as well, I believe. I wonder who will dance with whom?'

That evening, Flora's sketches were very much admired. The picture of Matthew – the contours of which Flora had carefully softened – was pronounced to be very like, the earl even going so far as to say that it was the best likeness of his cousin that he had ever seen.

'You have a keen eye, Miss Chayter,' he said. 'You must have observed my cousin very closely.' Flora listened carefully, and could detect no sarcasm in his tone, but he did not smile as he spoke. Flora's landscape was also admired, and Catherine declared her intention of going out herself soon to see whether she could achieve something in the same style. While the possibility of finding time for this was being discussed, Matthew found the chance to have a few words with Flora.

'Will you take Catherine up tonight?' he asked her in an undertone. 'Cosette has said that she will meet me in the garden if she should chance to be free, so. . . .'

'So it is up to me to see that she is free? Matthew, I told you to be cautious.'

'Yes I know, and I will be. But you promised to help.'

Conscious of the earl's steady gaze upon them and anxious to draw the exchange to a close, Flora said hurriedly, 'Very well, you foolish boy. But if you are not back by the time I have settled Catherine, I shall come to fetch you.'

'You're an angel,' he said, squeezing her hand impulsively. Shortly afterwards, Flora offered to take Catherine up to bed, saying that she was feeling a little tired herself. When they reached Catherine's room, Cosette was waiting outside.

'I can help Catherine tonight if you have something else that you wish to do,' Flora said. Cosette blushed and her radiant expression convinced Flora that the feeling between her and Matthew was certainly mutual.

'What is it that Cosette wishes to do?' asked Catherine after the Frenchwoman had gone.

'I think she needs to speak to someone,' replied Flora,

thankful that she need not tell a lie.

After Catherine was in bed, Flora walked along the passage to Cosette's room, and knocked on the door, but there was no reply, and when she looked inside, it was empty. Sighing, she made her way downstairs. If the attachment between them proved to be lasting, then the earl would have to know. His displeasure would be very much lessened if it were revealed that the courtship had been conducted in a seemly manner. Once downstairs, she walked down the little corridor that led to the pleasant garden at the back of the inn. There were a few trees planted there, some of them in bloom, and a wooden seat near the bottom, which was where Flora assumed the couple would be conducting their tryst. She had only gone halfway down the garden, however, when she came suddenly upon the figure of Lord Craythorne, engaged in the act of taking snuff. She gave a tiny gasp which caused him to turn round.

'Miss Chayter!' he exclaimed. 'I thought you intended to retire.' He sounded surprised, but not displeased.

'Yes I did,' she answered, thankful that the darkness was concealing her blushes. 'But it was such a lovely evening that I thought I would come and enjoy the fresh air.'

'It is a lovely night isn't it?' he replied. 'Look at the stars.' Flora looked up. Away from the glow of light from the half-open door, they stood out bright and clear against the night sky.

'Are they the same stars that we would see if we were in England?' she asked him.

'You mean the knowledgeable Miss Chayter does not know?' he murmured; but his tone was teasing, not unkind. 'I trust you are not feeling homesick for England?'

'Not at all,' she remarked. 'All those who are dear to me are here with me.' She looked away from the night sky and back at him then; and for a moment or two, she found it difficult to breathe.

'Are they?' he said softly.

Suddenly anxious to fill the silence, she said quickly, 'I am very much enjoying the chance to have new experiences and see new places.'

'I am glad that the tour is equal to your expectations,' he said courteously, and seemed about to turn back towards the inn. Behind him, Flora caught a glimpse of the movement of Cosette's gown, and quickly said, 'Wait, My Lord.'

'Miss Chayter?'

'Er . . . did you have a pleasant visit today?' She could have cursed herself for asking such a lame question, but it was all that she could think of to detain him.

'Very pleasant, thank you, ma'am, but I believe I mentioned that at table tonight.'

'D . . . did you?'

'Mm.'

'Oh. It . . . it must have been very agreeable for you to . . . to meet someone you knew.'

The earl smiled quizzically. 'As you say, Miss Chayter; although meeting people one knows can sometimes be a bit of a mixed blessing, as I'm sure you'll agree. Shall we go in now, or is there something else you wish to say to me out here – in the darkness?' Flora had no idea how to reply to this, so she was very relieved when Matthew appeared from the gloom at the bottom of the garden, saying, 'What a fine evening.'

'It is indeed,' replied Craythorne. 'I am beginning to wonder how many other persons might be wandering about here in the darkness.' His tone was jocular, his manner relaxed, so Flora could have kicked Matthew when he said at once, and in a rather defensive manner, looking at Flora as he did so, 'No one else, upon my honour.'

The earl looked at him in surprise, but he made no further comment on the matter, saying merely, 'In that case, let us go inside,' in a curt tone which seemed to indicate that his good mood was over, at least for the present.

The following evening, Mrs Wylde and Flora dressed very carefully, helped by Cosette and Catherine, who seemed very conscious of the importance of the occasion. Letty looked elegant in a gown of green satin, and Flora, making use of another of Jane's altered dresses, looked charming in blue. Both Matthew and the earl had made efforts with their appearance. Matthew was wearing purple, with a waistcoat of a lighter shade, and Craythorne, his hair powdered once more, looked magnificent in black with a silver figured waistcoat.

'Leigh looks very grand tonight – I wonder for whose benefit?' Letty whispered to Flora as they walked under the classically elegant portico of the *palazzo.*

Flora was to wonder the same on a number of different occasions during the course of the evening. The earl, as the guest of honour, was seated next to the *contessa.* and was seen to conduct several animated conversations with his hostess during the meal. When the time for dancing came, he was the first to lead her on to the floor, and acquitted himself with vigour, if not exactly grace.

Flora had not expected to dance very much. In the way of aristocratic assemblies everywhere, this particular gathering had soon managed to work out her status, and consequently, she was judged not to be a prize worth pursuing. But she was still a pretty girl, and she had a few partners, and she never lacked for someone to talk to when it was discovered that her Italian was fluent. Sadly, many of those talking to her were trying to find out about the earl's situation: was he single, were his estates vast, would he like to spend part of the year in Italy, and so on. She was heartily thankful when Matthew emerged from the card room and asked her to dance.

'Thank goodness,' she said as they took to the floor. 'At least you will not be interrogating me about Lord Craythorne's prospects.'

'Leigh's prospects? Good heavens! Is that what the old dowagers have been asking you about?'

Flora nodded. 'Though what I'm supposed to know, I can't imagine. Why don't they ask you?'

'Ah, but I've thought of the perfect ploy,' replied Matthew. 'If I don't like the question, I pretend that I don't understand. Being fluent in another language is always praised, but I've always thought it to be something of a drawback – it leaves you with absolutely no excuses at all.' Flora laughed. Moments later, the movement of the dance meant that she was facing the earl and the *contessa.* They were dancing together as if they were made for one another. For some reason that Flora could not have explained, this meant that she found herself talking to Matthew with more animation than ever. But somehow, inside, her heart felt as if it was at the bottom of her kid slippers.

Chapter Ten

'I must say, it is very agreeable to be in a coach and stretch out a little instead of on one of those wretched mules,' said Mrs Wylde once they were settled inside another hired coach, and the others heartily agreed with her. Lord Craythorne had once more hired horses for himself and his cousin, and the two men spent most of their time in the saddle, although it must be said that Matthew seemed to choose to sit inside more than heretofore. On these occasions, Flora tried to occupy Catherine's and Letty's attention, so that Matthew and Cosette might enjoy one another's company, and she was often rewarded by Matthew with a squeeze of the hand, or by Cosette with a grateful smile.

It soon became apparent to them all that travelling in Italy was not the straightforward business that it had been in France. Every town and area appeared to have its own regulations regarding passports and the possession and transport of goods, and nothing could ever be achieved without greasing the fist of every official encountered on the journey.

'Really, Leigh!' exclaimed Mrs Wylde, after money had changed hands yet again on their arrival at Milan. 'This is quite absurd! We will be penniless by the time we reach Jane's house at this rate!'

'Not at all,' answered the earl. It was one of the few occasions when he had chosen to ride in the coach for a change. 'I had allowed for all this in my provision for the journey.'

'I must say I am very surprised,' grumbled Mrs Wylde. 'I had not supposed you to be the kind of man to submit to petty officialdom.'

'I prefer to deal with situations as they are, rather than as I would like them to be,' he replied. 'Refusal to comply would simply result in a costly delay. The bribes I hand out add up to a fraction of what it would cost us in extra nights' lodging if I refused to pay up.'

It had become a custom amongst them on arrival at a new place to meet after their meal and talk about future plans. Since their departure from Paris, this had been a time to which Flora had begun to look forward, now that she was no longer living under the cloud of the earl's disapproval. On their first evening in Milan, he seemed perhaps a little more reserved than normal, but perfectly courteous, and very ready to listen to everybody's opinions.

'We will stay here for a few days, I think,' he said, smiling at Letty. 'Some of us need to recover still further from the rigours of our mountain adventure, and there is plenty to see.' Mrs Wylde looked relieved.

'Yes, by all means let us rest here a while,' she declared with a sigh, for all the world as if she had had to traverse the mountains on her own feet. 'What would you recommend we look at?'

'We must visit the theatre,' put in Mr Warren. 'I believe it is the largest in the world.'

Catherine's eyes grew wide. 'May we go and see the play, Craythorne?' she asked.

'By all means,' replied her uncle. 'And I think we should also visit the cathedral.'

'Is it true that it is still not finished – after nearly four centuries?' asked Flora.

'I believe so,' answered the earl courteously but briefly. 'As for the other sights, there is the Ambrosian library, which has a fine collection. . . .' Here Matthew Warren cast up his eyes and struck his brow in imitation of one of the inn servants, whose task it had been to help carry in their luggage, including the box which contained their books. Everyone laughed, except for the earl, who merely smiled slightly. He went on, '. . . I repeat, it has a fine collection worthy of the perusal of those not too ignorant to appreciate it.' Matthew shook his hand as if it were hot, and Flora had to smile, even while she tried to look disapproving. The earl's brows drew together in something like his well-remembered scowl from earlier on in the journey. 'Is there any value in continuing this discussion, or would you rather talk nonsense all evening?' he asked.

'No please, go on, Uncle,' said Catherine laying a hand on his arm. 'It is all so exciting.' Then realizing what she had said, she hurriedly corrected herself. 'Oh, I beg your pardon, Craythorne.' He smiled at her, his gaze softening.

'It's all right, Catherine,' he said. 'Call me Uncle if you really wish to do so, but not "Uncle Craythorne", I beg of you. Or you may call me Leigh, as Letty and Matthew do.'

'May I really?' she asked. She turned to Flora as if to say something, then stopped herself. There was a short silence in which Flora realized that she was the only one of their intimate little group who had not been invited to call the earl by his Christian name. To cover the awkward moment, she said quickly, 'Are there other sights for us to see while we are here, My Lord?' Then she blushed as she remembered that she had addressed him by the title which everyone else was permitted to drop.

'If Letty can bear the idea of a boat trip, we can visit the Borromaean palace, in the centre of Lake Maggiore on the Isola Bella,' he replied.

'A boat trip on a lake!' exclaimed Mrs Wylde 'Now that

sounds exactly the kind of outing that I might enjoy.'

The following day, it was arranged that the party would split into two. Mrs Wylde was anxious to look around the shops, and the earl, when told of the proposed expedition, shook his head in exasperation.

'My dear Letty, I bring you halfway across Europe and you want to go shopping! I dare swear the shops will be no better than any you might find in Bond Street, and probably not as good.'

'Perhaps not,' she retorted. 'But they will be different.'

Flora, knowing that any spending money she might have would be provided out of Mrs Wylde's purse, felt that she would rather not go shopping, so she turned to Catherine and said, 'What would you like to do today? Do you want to go shopping?' Catherine, to whom a book was always preferable to a ribbon, gave a quick but polite denial.

'I would prefer to visit the library that my uncle mentioned last night,' she said.

'The Ambrosian library,' said His Lordship, in gratified tones. 'By all means; unless Letty had rather we waited until another day, when she is free.'

'Certainly not,' said Mrs Wylde hurriedly. 'I would not have you postpone your pleasure on my account. And what of you, Flora? Will you shop with us or go to the library?'

'I had rather go to the library if you don't mind.' replied Flora, colouring a little.

'Then in that case, I hope no one will object if I take Cosette with me,' said Letty. 'That girl has an excellent eye for colour.'

'And you, Matthew?' asked Craythorne.

'Perhaps each group should have a man with them,' he replied, colouring only slightly. 'I will go shopping with Letty.'

'Very well then,' said the earl, whose sunny good nature seemed to have reappeared. 'We will meet later, and judge which of us has spent his time more profitably.'

The Ambrosian library was well worth seeing, housing as it did a fine collection of medals and sculpture, as well as some of the mechanical drawings of Leonardo Da Vinci, in addition to the precious manuscripts and books within its walls.

Catherine was fascinated with the drawings, and with the notes that went with them, indecipherable until the curator showed her how the writing could be made out by use of a mirror, for Leonardo had written backwards. Flora could see that she was taken with the idea, and hoped that she would not be so fascinated that she would want to make use of it in her own writing.

'Don't worry,' said the earl, surprising her by his sensitivity to her thoughts. 'I'm sure it will prove to be a short-lived craze. Do you wish to linger here, or shall we examine some of the early texts in their keeping?'

Flora opted to look at early texts, so once they were sure that Catherine was happy where she was, and that the curator would bring her to them when she was ready, they went in search of early writings and were soon being shown a copy of Vergil which had once belonged to Petrarch, and in which he had inscribed his own notes.

'If the *signor* and the *signorina* would care to look closely, they will see that here in the margin. . . .'

'Yes, I see,' said Flora eagerly, translating for herself. 'He writes of the first time he met Laura. See here, My Lord.'

'One moment,' said the earl, taking from his pocket a pair of spectacles. 'You have discovered my weakness, you see,' he said wryly. 'If the text is very small, or difficult to read.' The two of them examined it carefully.

'To think that this has been written for over four hundred years,' murmured Flora in wonderment. 'The moment when he fell in love preserved for all time, to be read here and now by us.' She turned her head to look at him, and saw that he had taken off his glasses and was already looking at her steadily.

Simultaneously they realized how close together they were, and Flora stepped back hurriedly. 'I am being greedy,' she said. 'You must take a turn to examine it closely, My Lord.'

'There are many other manuscripts to look at,' said the librarian. 'If the *signorina* would care to see a manuscript of Flavius Josephus, then it can be arranged, but it is one of our greatest treasures and must be treated carefully.'

Flora readily assented, and was very impressed with the valuable document, and with all that she saw that day. But, somehow, the memory of how she and Craythorne had stood so close together and pored over Petrarch's copy of Vergil was the one that stayed in her mind.

The visit to the Borromaean palace was judged to be too time-consuming to be indulged in on this occasion. Although Mrs Wylde appeared to be all complaisance, she was really quite anxious to get to Venice in order to see Jane and be with her before the baby arrived. They all agreed that the boat trip on Lake Maggiore could very well wait until their return journey, for they had learned that there was so much to be seen on the island that it was really necessary to stay there for several days in order to experience it all.

The following day was to be their last in Milan, and as it was unthinkable to miss seeing the cathedral or the theatre, they decided to visit the cathedral in the morning, rest and prepare for their departure in the afternoon, and attend a performance at the theatre in the evening.

Even Matthew was persuaded to look round the Duomo, and he acted very nobly as Flora's escort for quite ten minutes, dutifully admiring the gloomy dignity of the place, and examining with rather more interest the silver statue of Carlo Borromeo. But his interest soon waned, and when he had looked at his watch for the fourth time in as many minutes, Flora half laughing, half in exasperation, urged him to go elsewhere.

'By no means,' he declared gallantly. 'My place is here with you.'

'It's quite all right,' said Flora. 'The beggars don't alarm me. I haven't any money and I know how to tell them so. Lord Craythorne and Letty are here in this very building. Now do go along and amuse yourself somewhere else.'

After only a token further protest, he took his leave, hurrying off to walk about in the sunshine and possibly, Flora suspected, to go in search of Cosette. Once he had gone, she found herself able to relax much more, to admire at her leisure the lofty proportions of the building, and to allow her mind to imagine the many worshippers who had bowed the knee within it.

As she was contemplating one of the windows, she became conscious of someone at her elbow, and she looked round, expecting to find that Matthew Warren had returned. Her consternation was therefore so much the greater when she realized that it was Malcolm Brenner.

'Good heavens,' she said faintly, for he was certainly the last person on earth whom she had expected to see. He did not seem to be similarly amazed and his composure was explained by his first utterance.

'I thought it was you,' he said. 'I've been watching you for the past few minutes. Is Craythorne here?'

'Yes, somewhere,' answered Flora, looking round. 'If you want to speak to him. . . .'

'Heaven forbid,' replied Malcolm, blanching perceptibly, so that Flora could see it, even in the dim light of the cathedral. 'Look, can we find somewhere to talk?'

He put his hand under her elbow, and fairly pulled her along until they reached a secluded recess, unlikely to be found by any other visitors. They sat down and Flora looked at him expectantly, and with not a little annoyance.

'I hope this is important, after you have practically dragged me over here,' she said tartly.

After a short silence, during which he sat looking at his clasped hands, he looked up at her face and said, 'Flora, you've got to help me.' She looked across at him and wondered how she could ever have fancied herself in love with him. His merry blue eyes now seemed calculating, his mouth wilful, his chin weak. She regarded him steadily, without speaking, and he had the grace to look away, ashamed. 'You're right of course,' he went on. 'I have no right to expect any kind of help from you after the way I treated you.'

'Well I'm glad you realize that,' retorted Flora.

'Believe me, I wouldn't turn to you unless I couldn't think of another way. But you see, I'm desperate.'

Flora sighed. 'Very well, then, you had better tell me,' she said. 'But I cannot promise to help you until I know what sort of trouble you are in.'

He swallowed, then said baldly, 'I've eloped.'

'Eloped?' Flora was so surprised that her voice came out louder than she had intended. 'With whom?' she added in a much softer voice.

'With the sweetest, prettiest . . .' he began, then remembering the exact circumstances under which he and Flora had last met, he broke off what he was saying and took hold of Flora's hand. 'Flora, you must know that I left you entirely against my will,' he said urgently. 'I didn't want to do so, but the pressure Craythorne exerted. . . . Flora, he is a powerful man and a dangerous one. His threats were such that I had to leave for both our sakes; but I must not say more on that head. The point is that I tore myself away from your side. I set off to go to my estate at Brywood, but stopped on the way at Leamington. It was there that I met her.' He fell silent, as if contemplating some beautiful, inner vision.

'Her?' prompted Flora, pulling her hand away. She was disgusted by his protestations, but could not help but be interested in his tale almost despite herself.

'Marietta. I intended to stay in Leamington just for a night or two. I found quite by chance that a couple of good fellows were staying there, and . . . but never mind that,' he concluded hastily, adding fuel to Flora's speculation that he had indulged in some more gambling which he could ill afford. 'I met Marietta at an assembly. She was an Italian girl, visiting some English relatives. The intention had been that she should have a London season, but she had fallen prey to some childish complaint and so was spending some time in Leamington recuperating. I told her all about you, Flora, and about how we had been cruelly parted by my devil of a cousin. She was so sympathetic, so kindly and interested. . . .'

'. . . That you fell out of love with me and into love with her almost on the spot,' said Flora conversationally.

'No!' protested Malcolm. 'Not on the spot. It took me quite three days to realize what she had come to mean to me. I meant to woo her properly, in form, but my cursed ill luck still seemed to dog me.'

If Flora considered that his cursed ill luck which had blessed him with good looks, money to spare, and time to be idle and which still seemed to ensure that girls were drawn to him like moths to a flame was not really that bad, then she held her peace on that score, saying merely, 'What happened, then?'

'Oh, I had nearly convinced – that is, made plain to Marietta's chaperon the extent of my feelings, when bloo— when Robert Harland turned up with that loose-tongued mother of his.'

'And they are?'

'Only some of Craythorne's closest friends! It didn't take them more than a day to start spreading the dirt about me. Before twenty-four hours had passed, I found myself forbidden to speak to Marietta.'

'So what did you do?' asked Flora, knowing the answer before she had even asked the question.

'What could I do? Much against my will, I decided that we had better elope.'

'And have done so,' agreed Flora. 'So what is your difficulty now?' Inwardly, she prepared herself for a demand for money that she would certainly not be able to meet.

'Well you see, her family have taken against me,' he confided, sensing victory. 'They don't realize that I have an old distinguished name, and a property, and they think that I'm just an adventurer. Marietta's got plenty of money, but. . . .'

'I see,' replied Flora, inwardly congratulating Marietta's family on their perspicacity. 'You don't expect me to give you any money, I hope.'

'Well, not unless . . .' he began, then took one look at her face and finished virtuously, 'no, of course not!'

'I really cannot see what help I can be to you,' said Flora frankly.

'I thought you might put in a good word for me,' he said coaxingly.

'I? But what possible influence could I have? I am just a governess-companion on this journey. Why should a distinguished Italian family take any notice of me?'

'Not with them – with Craythorne.'

'Craythorne?' She stared at him in disbelief. 'No! I cannot credit this! You seriously expect me to plead your case with Lord Craythorne?'

'Well, why not? He's high enough in the instep to impress them.' He put on his coaxing tone once again. 'I can't tell you how surprised I was when I discovered quite by chance that you were of his party here in Milan! You must be well in with him, that's obvious. Otherwise, why would he have brought you with him on the Continent? Whatever you said to him after I left must have been pretty appealing!'

Flora looked at him in stunned silence. She had long since accepted that his desertion of her on that fateful night at Mrs

Brenner's had revealed his selfish nature; but she had not dreamed that his effrontery could possibly lead him to be so utterly insensitive to her feelings as his words were now revealing.

'I can't believe it!' she exclaimed at last in tones of amazement. 'You left me alone to face his wrath, with never a thought to the consequences to me, whatever you may say. Would you like to know what happened after you left? He dismissed me, Malcolm! I am at present in the employ of Mrs Wylde, and not of the earl. In fact, whatever you may choose to have surmised, he barely tolerates my presence most of the time, because of what our conduct led him to believe about me. What exactly do you think would be his reaction if I now go to him with tales of your . . .' she paused, to find the right phrase, and finally concluded with, 'your *romantic adventures*?'

Even Malcolm Brenner's supreme self-satisfaction appeared to be dented a little by this thought. He pondered for a moment.

'Well, of course, you couldn't rush straight in with the whole story,' he admitted, and appeared about to continue. Flora got hastily to her feet.

'I have absolutely no intention of rushing, ambling, or tiptoeing in with any part of it,' she said forthrightly. 'Your effrontery knows no bounds! As for approaching Lord Craythorne on your behalf, I had rather walk back to England barefoot.' At this, his expression changed to one of irritation, as he realized that Flora was firm in her decision.

'You always were a cold piece – at least with me,' he added with a sneer. 'I wonder how you're really paying for the cost of your transport here?'

Flora did not immediately grasp his meaning, and she said firmly, 'I have already told you that I am in the employ of Mrs Wylde.'

'Oh yes, so you say,' he retorted. 'You wouldn't have me in

your bed – so virtuous as you were! I'll wager you couldn't wait once His rich Lordship crooked his little finger!' Flora blushed as she fully grasped the import of what he was saying.

'You're beneath contempt,' she replied. 'I would slap your face, but I don't want to soil my hands. Kindly refrain from speaking to me again, either on this subject, or on any other.' So saying, she hurried back into the main body of the church. He made no attempt to detain her, but paused briefly before taking the same route. Flora was just looking round for the rest of the party, when she heard her name spoken and turned to see Mr and Mrs Sharman, a pleasant couple who had only arrived at the inn the previous night. They were on their way back to England, and had stopped to spend a few days in Milan.

'Miss Chayter, are you finding the cathedral interesting?' asked Mrs Sharman. 'It is our second visit, but we felt that we did not take it all in the last time.' At this moment, Malcolm Brenner walked past, bowed slightly to Flora, then walked away, carefully avoiding the main entrance. Flora acknowledged his bow with an inclination of her head, and though Mrs Sharman looked a little curious, she made no attempt to enlighten her. The three of them walked along together and within a few minutes, they met up with Lord Craythorne, Catherine and Mrs Wylde. With the person of Malcolm Brenner fresh in her mind, Flora could not help but compare his ingratiating demeanour with the earl's self-possessed assurance. They walked out into the sunshine, and as they stepped outside, Flora looked at the earl again. He was not handsome – he would never be that – but there was a healthy manliness about him that contrasted strongly with Malcolm's complexion, which was already beginning to acquire the sickliness of the hardened gamester. The difference between them tugged at her heartstrings in a way that she did not yet feel confident enough to investigate.

As they strolled back to the inn, Craythorne remembered that he had reserved a box for them at the opera that night and wondered whether Mr and Mrs Sharman might like to join them.

'Catherine will stay with Cosette, I think,' he said, 'But my cousin Mr Warren will accompany us I am sure.' He turned to Flora. 'By the way, Miss Chayter, he was supposed to have been looking after you inside the cathedral. Never tell me that he basely deserted you!'

'That must have been the young man I saw you with,' remarked Mrs Sharman. 'If so, I can assure you, My Lord, that he left the cathedral only a few minutes before we met you.'

Flora opened her mouth to say something, then closed it again. They were leaving Milan the following day, and she had made it quite plain enough to Malcolm that he had nothing to gain from hanging about their party. In any case, she could not possibly speak about him in front of strangers. Any account of the morning's doings would have to be given to the earl in private.

Privacy with His Lordship was not to prove possible however. Mrs Wylde was beginning to feel the glimmerings of a headache, so Flora promised to go with her to her room and arrange for a tisane to be prepared. While that was happening, the earl took Catherine for a walk, then later he paid a visit to the bankers who were accommodating him in Milan, and before any chance of an explanation had occurred, it was time to dress for dinner.

Whilst Mrs Wylde slept off her headache, Flora sat and brooded about her encounter, wondering whether it would be best to tell the earl or not. She had to admit that part of her reluctance to mention it lay in the fact that she had no wish to resurrect an episode that threw her character into such a bad light.

No opportunity presenting itself either before dinner or

afterwards, she went along to the opera with the rest of the party, still wondering whether to say anything or to try to forget about the whole incident.

Matthew had briefly made an appearance at the inn, but he had made his excuses concerning dinner as by chance he had bumped into an old college friend and they were going to spend some time together. He would, however, join them at the opera after he had kept his appointment.

Flora had never visited the theatre before, so had nothing with which to compare her visit in Milan, but Mrs Wylde's excited exclamations and the earl's more measured agreements served to convince her that the theatre here was indeed beyond the common. The very entrance itself was stately and grand, and inside, the splendour of the silk hangings and the gilding was enough to take her breath away.

'My dear, I can assure you that Covent Garden is nothing to it – nothing at all!' declared Mrs Wylde when they were settled in their box. 'My dear Leigh, we should have brought Cosette after all, for I see that there is a little chamber just across the corridor from this where she could have made drinks for us!'

Mr and Mrs Sharman were also full of admiration and declared themselves delighted to have had the opportunity of visiting the theatre before their return.

Matthew Warren had still not appeared and Flora wondered how he would find them in the crowd, but she soon ceased to be concerned when the music began, and she turned her attention to the stage. When the break in the performance came she was astonished to see how much time had passed, so captivated had she been by what she had witnessed. She looked round at her companions, her face aglow, and surprised on Craythorne's face an answering smile of such sweetness that her heart skipped a beat.

'Shall we go and walk about a little?' he suggested. His words were for the whole party, but his look was just for her, and suddenly she began to glimpse what it might be like to be cherished by such a man. Mrs Wylde decided to stay in the box, but Mr and Mrs Sharman both wanted a little exercise so they left the box together. As they gained the corridor, Mrs Sharman said suddenly, 'Oh look, Lord Craythorne, there is your cousin.' There was quite a press of persons where she was pointing and the earl scanned the crowd, looking for the familiar dark curly hair so like his own.

'I think not,' he replied courteously.

'Yes, there he is,' responded Mrs Sharman. 'Just there, that fair young man. That was the gentleman with whom you were conversing in the cathedral, was it not Miss Chayter?'

There came over Lord Craythorne a sudden rigid stillness as he recognized Malcolm Brenner; at the same time, Brenner looked at him, so that their gaze locked, slate-grey eyes boring into apprehensive blue ones. Then, as someone walked between them and the moment was broken, Craythorne turned his head to look at Flora, and she could feel herself turning scarlet.

'Ah yes, it is as you say,' he said, speaking to Mrs Sharman, but still looking at Flora in a way which seemed to wipe out all the friendly exchanges that they had ever had, and take them right back to the nadir of their relationship. Then he bowed slightly to the whole party. 'Excuse me, if you please, I must go and talk to my – cousin.' He walked over to Malcolm and took him by the elbow, and the two men disappeared down the corridor. Moments later, a diversion was created when Matthew Warren came hurrying up.

'Miss Chayter! Forgive me! I am so late! But you look rather pale. Are you well? Let me escort you back to your box and procure a drink for you.'

'Thank you,' said Flora in a small voice. 'I am well. Just a little tired. I would be glad to sit down.' Then, remembering her manners, she introduced him to the Sharmans. They looked a little puzzled that the earl had not mentioned having two cousins in Milan, but Flora did not think about that until much later. Her mind was too full of the transformation that she had seen in Craythorne from easy good humour to the same kind of cold rigidity that had characterized his manner to her earlier in the trip.

The rest of the opera passed her by entirely. Craythorne did not return, and Matthew escorted them all back to the inn later. She was even spared having to make up excuses for the earl's absence, for Mrs Wylde was too full of the experience to take in any more than Mrs Sharman's comment that she thought he had discovered an appointment which he needed to keep.

Much later that night, Flora woke from an uneasy sleep thinking that she had heard unsteady footsteps on the stairs and in the passage, and a door opening, but she might have been mistaken.

Chapter Eleven

The following day, when they all met at the breakfast table, the atmosphere had lost its relaxed nature, and had regained the feeling of tension that had been a mark of the early days of their tour. The earl's eyes, when they met those of Flora, were as cold and contemptuous as she had ever seen them.

'Unfortunately, a matter of business has come up,' he announced to them all in general, 'and I am obliged to stay on in Milan for a few days until it is settled. Matthew will escort you very ably, as I know that you want to travel on, Letty. I will ride after you as soon as my business is concluded.'

'Oh Craythorne!' exclaimed Catherine, forgetting in her disappointment to drop the old form of address. 'It won't be nearly as good without you.' For the first time since he had sat down, the earl's expression softened.

'Never fear, I'll catch you up soon enough,' he replied. As the meal drew to a close, he stood up. 'If you will excuse me, I will be about my business. You will be gone by the time I return, so I will say goodbye now.' He had a hug for Catherine, a handshake for his cousin, and a courteous bow for Mrs Wylde.

For Flora, there was only a curt nod. Knowing that this would be her last opportunity, she said desperately, 'My Lord, if I might just have a word with you. . . .'

'No, Miss Chayter, you may not,' he replied shortly, and immediately walked to the door. In her anxiety to correct any misunderstanding, she hurried out of the room after him and into the corridor, heedless of how her actions might be interpreted by the other members of the party.

'My Lord . . .' she began again. He had not realized that she had followed him, and he turned to face her, his expression a mixture of surprise, fury and contempt. In the confined space of the passage, he seemed to tower over her.

'I said no, madam,' he snarled. 'You forfeited the right to speak with me when you agreed to meet Brenner clandestinely. And to think that I had begun to trust you! What a fool I was to believe you! Well you have had your last chance. As soon as I have dealt with your paramour, I shall set about making arrangements for you to return to England immediately. My family can do without the pollution of your presence.'

Horrified at what she was hearing, Flora tried once more. 'I beg of you . . .' she began.

'For the final time, no I say!' he declared. 'Is that so difficult to understand? Or is "no" a word that you are not accustomed to hearing from a man?' She shrank back before him then, and watched as he left the inn, slamming the door behind him.

In the bustle of preparing for their departure, no one had noticed what had taken place between them, but the earl's change of mood had been plain to all, and later that day, when they stopped at Lodi for the night, Matthew asked her if she thought that anything was amiss.

'Amiss?' asked Flora, her attempt at airy unconcern sounding unconvincing even to herself. She glanced over to the other side of the room where Mrs Wylde was teaching Catherine a new embroidery stitch. They were unlikely to be overheard in this larger than average private room.

'Well, you must have noticed the way that Leigh suddenly changed his tune today. He's been so relaxed and good-humoured. Then suddenly today he pokered up again. Wouldn't give me any inkling of the business that is keeping him in Milan, either, and that's unusual. I wondered whether it was anything to do with the fact that I was so late for the opera last night?' An expression of anxiety crossed his face. 'You don't suppose he's got wind of my interest in Cosette, do you?' Flora looked at his worried countenance and remembered that Matthew was also his cousin's secretary, and was therefore probably accustomed to knowing about all his business concerns. Trying to forget her own troubles, she hurriedly reassured him.

'I am certain that he has not,' she said truthfully. 'Perhaps someone at the opera had a commission for him which he was bound to keep confidential, even from you.'

'Perhaps so,' agreed Matthew. 'But whatever the commission may have been, it certainly gave him no pleasure. I do not think I have seen his brow so black since before Paris.' Flora murmured something non-committal, and presently Matthew went on, 'I am aware that you do not have much cause to love my cousin, Flora, but I can assure you that the man you have seen since we left Paris is much more the man that I know. We are not closely related, but a kinder and more concerned relative I could not hope to have. That is, not to say kind in a milky sort of way, but aware of real needs, and realistic in the help that he offers.'

'I must say that I have found him to be rather hasty in his judgements at times,' she replied feelingly.

'Yes, he can be,' answered Matthew with a rueful grin. 'But annoyingly enough, he is often right!'

Not about me, thought Flora to herself. At this point, Catherine came over to show them what she had done, and the conversation proceeded no further.

After Lodi, their journey took them through Cremona, Mantua, Verona and Vicenza. At each place they stayed for one night, and at Vicenza they stayed for two, partly because it was Sunday, and Mrs Wylde did not approve of Sunday travelling, and partly because they wanted to admire some of the buildings designed by Palladio. There was much to look at and take in wherever they went, but always for Flora, there seemed to be a sword of Damocles hanging over her head as she waited for the earl to catch them up. Undoubtedly the business detaining him in Milan had been that of Malcolm.

From the brief, violent conversation that she had had with Craythorne, it was plain that far from assuring the earl of the coincidental nature of their meeting, Malcolm had encouraged him to place the worst possible construction upon the encounter. Flora was at a loss to understand such vindictiveness. She could only assume that it was partly because she had refused to help him, and partly because Malcolm thought that the earl had succeeded with her where he had failed. Some chance! she thought to herself, then wondered why she should put it in such a way.

When they had first left Milan, anger at the injustice of Craythorne's low opinion of her had buoyed up her spirits. Now, as she dutifully admired the Villa Capra, she could only reflect on how much more enjoyable the outing would have been had the earl been with them. The idea that his sense of disgust for her would now be so great that such companionship would now only be a distant memory took hold of her and she was filled with an aching sense of loss. She was unable to think of a reason for this until on their last evening at Vicenza, whilst out for a stroll, they came upon a pair of lovers entwined on the bank of the Brenta, totally oblivious to passers-by, the young woman willingly receiving the eager kisses of her swain.

After one glance, she looked away, but that night in bed, as she began to doze off, the scene came back to her mind. In her imagination, the lovers were herself and Lord Craythorne. Her eyes flew wide open in shock, and she half turned towards Mrs

Wylde, convinced that her thoughts must somehow have communicated themselves to her bed-fellow. Mrs Wylde merely murmured in her sleep and turned over, and Flora sighed, closed her eyes and tried to relax. Her pattern of sleep had been disturbed, however, and she found herself wide awake, with no longer the slightest feeling of tiredness. At last, feeling certain that the happy times with the earl were at an end, she allowed herself to think about him; his interest in all that they saw during their travels; his commanding presence; his swarthy face, not handsome, but quite unforgettable in the strength of his features; his dependability.

'Oh no!' she exclaimed out loud, causing Mrs Wylde to stir in her sleep. Fortunately, she soon settled down again, for had she woken and asked Flora for the reason for her exclamation, could Flora have found anything to say that was half so convincing as the truth: 'I have just discovered that I am in love with Lord Craythorne'? Matthew had been right days ago; Craythorne had given her no reason to love him; but she did love him all the same, and with a love that surely defied reason itself.

The next day brought them to Padua and there was nothing there that encouraged them to linger. The whole place seemed infected with an atmosphere of melancholy, ideally suited to Flora's present mood. It was not clean; the streets were ill-kept; and even the university no longer had the reputation that it had once possessed. They were obliged to linger there, however, for it was at Padua that they were to board a boat and float down the Brenta to Venice. Lord Craythorne had directed Matthew to keep the party at the inn until his arrival.

On their second day there, Mrs Wylde said, 'We might as well have a look around as we are here. Peter spent a short time at the university here when he was a young man. I would like to be able to tell him that I had taken a look at it.' The others readily agreed, and examined with interest the names of past students engraved in brass tablets around the walls.

After their visit, they were on their way back to the inn, when Catherine exclaimed, 'Oh dear, I have left my sketching pad behind! I think I must have put it down on a table in the great hall.'

'We can go back and get it,' said Matthew, but Flora, seeing a chance to be on her own – of which there had been very few over the past few days – said quickly, 'Let me go back. It is only a step, after all. You go on, and I will meet you at the inn.' Matthew looked as if he would remonstrate, but Flora said, 'It's quite all right, and besides, Aunt Letty looks a little tired. I will be with you before you know it.' She turned away towards the university even as she was speaking, so that Matthew was left with the choice of coming after her and deserting his other two charges, or leaving her to go alone.

'Be careful!' he called out, confirming her suspicion that he would feel it to be his duty to remain with Catherine.

This was what Flora had banked on. She retraced their steps, and easily found Catherine's sketch book, exactly where its owner had suggested it might be. On coming out of the university, she looked at it from the outside for a little while, and enjoyed the chance just to be herself, and not respond to the needs of anyone else. Quite soon, she decided that she had better return to the inn so as not to cause alarm, but when she went to take the street that would lead her directly there, she found that it was blocked as a cart had shed its load. Rather than wait and cause her friends further anxiety, she made up her mind to go down a road parallel to the one she should have taken. Her plan was to find a turning to take her to the right as soon as possible.

It soon became clear, however, that there was no such turning. Furthermore, she began to realize that she was reaching an unsalubrious part of the town with frightening rapidity. The streets now looked mean as well as shabby, and the stares that she was encountering looked threatening rather than simply curious. A scruffy beggar began to importune her, and in her haste to get away from him, she took a wrong turning, and found herself up a blind alley. Turning back, she discovered her passage barred by a group of half a dozen or so men, shabbily dressed and unshaven, regarding her in a decidedly measuring way. Thinking that she might buy them off with money, she fumbled with the strings of her reticule, only to remember that she had very little in it with which to bribe them. One of them snatched it from her so brutally that it hurt her finger, and another took hold of her by the arm. They drew closer and she could imagine no escape.

Suddenly, a voice of authority spoke from the entrance to the alley. The men turned to look, and in the gap that opened between them, Flora saw Lord Craythorne walking towards them, the skirts of his riding coat swinging about him, his black hair confined in a bow, his tricorne on his head.

'Let her go,' he said harshly. 'She is nothing to you.'

'Maybe not, but we keep what we find,' replied a thickset man who seemed to have constituted himself as leader. He was dark, although not as dark as the earl, and unshaven, and he wore, rather incongruously, a tie wig in reasonable condition – no doubt a piece of booty from a previous encounter.

'Even if what you find belongs to someone else?' asked the earl.

'Even more so then,' laughed the other. Craythorne took a handful of silver out of his pocket and threw it on to the floor.

'Then find that,' he said. Some of the men made as if to pick up the money, but the leader stopped them with a gesture.

'Is she worth so little to you?' he asked. 'What more do you have to offer?' The earl looked at Flora for a moment, and she wondered wildly whether he was considering leaving her in the alley. What price he might have offered she was never to know, for the leader of the brigands went on to say, 'Is she worth fighting for – or do you not want to soil your fine clothes?' There was a murmur of mocking laughter amongst the group.

'A fight?' asked the earl, his voice devoid of emotion.

'A fight, *signor*,' agreed the leader. He was no taller than the earl, but he was broad of shoulder, with large square hands, the backs of which were covered with dark hairs. 'If you win, then the girl is yours.'

'And if I lose?' said the earl.

'You go free – but we keep the girl.'

'Hand-to-hand, just the two of us – with no interference?'

'As you say, *signor*.'

Craythorne considered for a short moment. 'Very well,' he said at last. 'Let it be so.' Flora whitened and swayed a little. So he really did hold her in contempt!

'Agreed,' said the brigand chief. 'Let us prepare ourselves.' So saying, he began to remove his coat.

'You shall be my second,' said Craythorne, turning to Flora and handing her his hat and coat.

'You . . . you agreed that they could keep me,' she murmured.

'I shan't lose,' he replied. 'I have other plans for you. It's strangely ironical though, you must admit, that I should be obliged to fight for the honour of one who has none.' She straightened her back and looked directly at him.

'You are wrong, My Lord,' she said. There was no time for more, for the bandit leader was saying, 'Not ready yet, *signor*?' He had stripped to the waist and was even now removing his wig to reveal a thin scrub of hair on top of his head. With a sigh, Craythorne unbuttoned his shirt and handed it to Flora with the rest of his clothes.

'There is no end to the trouble you cause me, is there?' he said. The men standing around looked at him in a measuring way, as if they had expected that the breadth of his shoulders would prove to be due to the padding in his coat and the clever cut of his shirt. 'Very well,' said Craythorne to the bandit leader. 'Let us begin.' Grinning, his adversary shook his head, and pointed to the earl's hair.

'And your wig, *signor*,' he said. With his first grin of the encounter, Craythorne pulled the ribbon from his hair, handed it to Flora with a flourish, and shook his head so that his curly mane flew about his shoulders. Anyone joining the group at that moment would have been hard put to it to say which was the brigand. The men laughed, and a little of the tension was dispelled. It was only as the glint of silver in the dust caught Flora's eye that she was reminded of the deadly necessity for the earl to triumph in this dispute.

All the men stepped back to give the fighters space, and one of them pulled Flora back too. The bravo rocked to and fro on his feet, grinning and showing several missing teeth. Craythorne crouched much as he had in the doorway on the night when the mouse had been found, but this time, his hands were clenched in two purposeful fists, his left guarding his face, his right forward. Then the fight began.

Flora had never seen men fighting at close quarters before, and she found it quite impossible to judge who might be the victor. Craythorne had seemed very confident, but the other man was surely used to brawling every day, and he seemed every bit as tall and strong as the earl.

What Flora was not to know was that Craythorne was a keen amateur sportsman. During the journey across Europe, he had spent more time in the saddle than he had in the carriage, an ordeal only to be undertaken by the physically fit. At home, it was very uncommon for him to pass a day without some form of vigorous sporting activity. Even during their journey, he had found time for fencing and sparring, and he was commonly rated as being one of the finest amateur boxers in England, and someone with exceedingly good 'bottom'. It was not for nothing that he had made his boast to Flora.

For all his confidence, however, he did not make the mistake of underrating his opponent. The first few minutes of the contest, therefore, were spent by him in circling carefully and judging the strength, accuracy and speed of his adversary. There was a fair bit of calling out from those around who supposed that he was merely trying to avoid the fight, but he was oblivious to it, as he disciplined his mind to think of nothing but the task ahead of him.

Flora hardly dared watch. The fact that her virtue depended on the result had receded from her mind, and she could only think that the earl must not be hurt in this adventure. If the worst came to the worst, she was not defenceless, for Craythorne in handing her his coat, had managed to show her by placing her hand on top of it, the shape of a pistol in one of the pockets, but she was not at all sure of her ability to hit anything with it, if the need became urgent.

It soon became apparent, however, that Craythorne was in no danger of losing this bout. He was quicker on his feet than the other man, his blows, when they made contact, inflicted more damage, and he was quicker to recover. Finally the bravo, feeling his strength giving out, tried to end it all with one blow, and Flora involuntarily turned away. Moments later, she looked up to see the bandit leader sprawled on the ground, with Craythorne standing over him, his fists still clenched, his feet apart. His chin was arrogantly high, his eyes flashed, and his chest was heaving and glistening with sweat.

There was a murmur of approval from those around, an acknowledgement that the fight had been fair and that their leader had been beaten by a worthy opponent. A small crowd had gathered nearby, and one woman threw a pan of water over the ruffian on the ground, whilst another handed the earl a cup of wine which he drained and handed back to her.

The vanquished bandit shook his head, brushed the water out of his eyes, and said, 'Well then, you fought for her, aren't you going to claim your prize?' The earl looked at Flora as she still stood holding his clothes, then without another word, he pushed her up against the wall and kissed her long and hard, to the loud applause of those around. It was a fierce and demanding kiss, without love or tenderness, and given simply in order to stake his claim; and a further outlet of the energy which he had just expended. As he drew away from her, he looked at her with an expression that was unreadable, then called farewell to the crowd and took Flora firmly by the arm.

'Come,' he said. 'Their humour is good now, but we need to be away from this area as quickly as possible.' He guided her back along the streets that she had only recently travelled, and it was not until they were in a slightly more salubrious area that he stopped to put on the clothes that he had taken off. Flora handed him each item in silence. Only the ribbon from his hair seemed to have been mislaid.

The brief halt enabled her to get her breath back, for his brisk stride had made no allowances for her. She glanced at him surreptitiously as he tied his cravat in a careless knot. The touch of his lips upon hers had stirred her, but she could not help remembering the bitterness of their previous encounter. He may have kissed her, but he had uttered no words of love or forgiveness. At last, as they were treading more familiar ways, she ventured to say, 'My Lord, I have to thank you for. . . .'

'For coming to your aid?' He completed her sentence for her. 'I would expect to have a care for all those travelling in my party – however little they may deserve it.'

'It is very true, I should not have wandered into unfamiliar streets,' she agreed.

'I was not referring to that, Miss Chayter,' he replied. He did not sound as angry and contemptuous as he had done last time they had met in Milan. Flora wondered whether Malcolm had redeemed himself by admitting to Craythorne that their meeting had been an accident.

'How did you find me?' she ventured to ask.

'When Matthew arrived back at the inn with Letty and Catherine and told me that you had gone back to the university alone, I decided to come and look for you. Padua's reputation is not what it was, and you are far too pretty to be allowed to wander about on your own. I set off for the university and spotted you turning down the wrong street, so I followed you.'

'The street I should have taken was blocked by a cart,' she murmured. He had called her pretty again, and he still did not sound angry, but there was a tension about him, and he did not sound happy either; not in the way that he had been between Paris and Milan. She looked around and saw that although they had taken the road leading to the inn, they were now walking down to the Brenta. 'My Lord, the others,' she began.

'Yes, I know, but I want to talk to you,' he said. They paused near the river, and for what seemed a long time, he was silent. Then at last he said, 'Miss Chayter, I have never known what to do with you, but now I believe I have made a decision and I hope it will mean that I can again have peace of mind. I first met you at my sister's house, when, God help me, I thought you a charming and virtuous young woman. Then I found you behaving like a strumpet with Malcolm Brenner. With some regret, I decided to rid my family of the contamination of your presence, only to discover to my disgust that you were to be a member of my travelling party. And how did I discover it? Only when you flung yourself at me on the boat, thinking me to be Matthew! You then created a fuss and admittedly behaved well until we reached Paris.

'On reaching there you flirted madly with Saint-Croix and Matthew in turn – my best friend and my favourite relative. You protested your innocence, and I, like a fool, believed you; I really did.' He took a deep breath. 'After that, I decided that I must have been mistaken in you – that you really were the honourable young woman that you pretended to be. Even when I realized that you were drawing close to Matthew, I told myself that such a connection would be acceptable, and I was preparing to give you my blessing, despite. . . .' He stopped for a moment. 'Then I discovered that you had been meeting Malcolm Brenner on the sly.'

Until now, Flora had been silent, unable to grasp of what she was being accused. Now, she felt impelled to speak. 'No, My Lord, you are quite wrong!' she cried. 'I did not meet Malcolm on the sly! I did not know he was there!'

'A pity you kept silent about it then,' he replied with a sneer. 'Perhaps I would have found that easier to believe had you taken the opportunity to tell me of his presence, rather than leave me to discover it in the most public of settings. I have to say that the trifling with Matthew's affections I find it harder to forgive. Malcolm is as immoral as you are, whereas Matthew deserves better. Had the others not been present in Milan, I really think I might have strangled you there and then.'

'But My Lord,' interrupted Flora again, wanting to correct his mistaken impression about her relationship with Matthew, but he went on without allowing her to finish.

'However, since then my anger has had a chance to cool, and since then, Miss Virtuous Flora Chayter, I have had a chance to kiss you myself, and have a taste of what all the others have enjoyed. I've stopped being angry because I've decided no longer to expect anything like decent behaviour from you, and simply treat you as the strumpet you are.

'On arrival at Venice, we will all go and stay with Letty's daughter as arranged – after all, it would look very strange if we did not – then after a short while, you and I will leave the rest of them there – they will be in Matthew's care, and safely under Jane's roof – and we will return home, madam, by the same route. But this time, as my mistress, you will share my bed, and perhaps if I indulge in the pleasures that Malcolm has enjoyed, I might at last get you out of my blood!' So saying, he pulled her into his arms and kissed her, his lips firm and demanding on her own. For a split second, the feeling of being in his arms was so treacherously all that she had so foolishly dreamed about, that her body responded to him quite independently of her will, but then the implications of all that he had said hit her hard, and she tore herself from his grasp, stepped back and wiped her mouth with a hand that was not quite steady.

'How dare you?' she cried in a trembling voice. 'How can you insult me so?'

'Insult you? By God, that's rich, madam! That would only be possible where there are finer feelings to be offended.'

'And you are the only one with finer feelings, I suppose. And of course, the great and mighty Earl of Craythorne can never be mistaken, can he?'

'The mistake I made was in trusting you,' he said contemptuously. 'Fortunately, in a purely physical relationship, trust is not necessary.' The earl took a step towards her, but she recoiled.

'Don't touch me,' she hissed.

'Don't touch you?' he sneered. 'You were glad enough to receive my kisses just now.'

'I just forgot for a moment . . .' she began.

'Who I was?' he finished for her. 'Amongst so many, I'm not surprised. But don't be afraid; after you've been my mistress for a week or so, I think I'll have managed to tame your wayward memory.'

'Don't flatter yourself,' she spat at him. 'I'd as soon become the mistress of that ruffian you fought, as become yours. Your kisses make me sick, and I cannot think of a man whom I find quite as repulsive as I do you. Is that plain enough?' She turned to go, but he seized her arm in a painful grip. His face once more wore that familiar lowering expression.

'Understand this, madam. In no circumstances will I permit you to associate yourself with Catherine again. I will not have her innocence polluted. Beyond the normal conventions, you will have nothing more to do with her. Either you accede to my demands, or you find yourself another party and another protector when we reach Venice.'

'So be it,' she replied. 'As soon as we reach Venice, our ways part. It can hardly be soon enough for me. If I never see you again after that, I shall be supremely happy.' Again she turned to go, and again he seized her arm.

'One moment . . .' he began.

'No!' she cried. 'No more!' Then, her voice breaking, she said, 'Oh why did you have to spoil it?' Pulling herself free from him, she picked up her skirts and ran in the direction of the hotel. For a moment, he stood watching her, his face grim. Then he took the same route back, but at a slower pace.

Chapter Twelve

The following day, the party stepped aboard a *burchio*, which was to take them along the Brenta to Venice in about eight hours. This should have been an exciting episode in the tour, but the whole party was very subdued. Neither Lord Craythorne nor Flora spoke of their quarrel, but the tension between them hung in the air and affected the atmosphere to a marked degree. They stood at opposite ends of the barge and carefully avoided one another. It had not proved possible for her to cut herself off from Catherine completely, because Catherine herself, not knowing what had happened, had come to speak to her. Without being rude, Flora had managed to convey the impression that she was not feeling well, and Catherine had readily given her attention to her uncle.

In truth, Flora's excuse was not really an excuse at all. After her encounter with Craythorne the previous day, she had returned to the inn and had gone to her room, where she had remained. Mrs Wylde had tapped discreetly on the door, but Flora had pleaded a headache, and had stayed there until the morning, refusing the tray of dinner that was offered to her. Thankfully, this inn was more spacious than any other in which they had stayed and Flora had a room to herself, so her privacy was undisturbed.

For a time indignation had buoyed her up, but then with further reflection had come resentment of Malcolm, that once again his conduct should have ruined her reputation, and this time through no fault of her own. Coupled with this was a hurt despair that the earl should so easily think the worse of her, and finally, bitterness that despite everything, she could still feel love for Craythorne; a love which had always been foolish, and must now surely be hopeless. In her mind she went over and over the insulting speech that he had made to her. Never had she been spoken to in such a way!

'This time, as my mistress, you will share my bed', was what he had said. Although it was painful to admit it, his arrogant demands had tempted her as Malcolm's sugar-sweet insinuations had never done. She wondered whether she would have weakened despite her principles if he had made such a suggestion out of love. But knowing his low opinion of her, she could never succumb to him without losing her self respect, and there were times when, as a governess, she had felt that that was nearly all she had. No, she had made the right decision, and she had been right to upbraid him for his insults. No doubt the earl would now take up again with his *contessa* and make a suitable marriage, instead of indulging in a shabby liaison, and they would both be divinely happy. So why if her decision was the best thing for everyone, did tears come so readily and sleep refuse to come at all?

At last, in a grey dawn, she rose, dressed and went downstairs, desperate for some fresh air to clear her aching head. She walked out of the inn and into the street, unaware of the motionless figure standing at one of the upstairs windows.

Craythorne turned away abruptly and rubbed his unshaven chin. He had had nearly as little sleep as Flora, and what little he had had not refreshed him. He had dined with the rest of the party, but had been unable to keep his mind on the conversation, and on one occasion Letty had had to address him four times before he became aware of the need to answer her.

After the meal, he had excused himself from the company and had gone into another inn, less salubrious than the one in which they were staying, where he had drunk considerably more than was customary for him. Instead of cheering him up, the quantity he had drunk merely made him more and more morose, until those with whom he had chosen to drink were heartily glad when he removed himself together with the cloud that he was casting over the whole proceedings. On his return to the inn he was set upon by a couple of thieves, of whom he made short work and, as he knocked their heads together, he imagined them to be Malcolm and Flora.

On his arrival back at the inn, he had tumbled into bed and dozed fitfully for an hour or so, but he had woken in the middle of the night with a raging thirst, and a dim memory of the fragments of a dream in which he had made some colossal blunder which could not be put right. Once fully awake, he freshened himself with a drink of water, and still more of the same poured over his head. He tried to tell himself that the sense of guilt that he was feeling was simply a residue of the dream that he had had, but the nagging at his conscience would not go away, no matter how he told himself that his harsh words had been justified. He could call her as much of a trollop as he liked, but into his head there would keep coming her last words to him: 'Oh why did you have to spoil it?' and her white face as she had said them. After that, sleep was impossible and, as he stood at the window, he saw her leave the inn. An assignation, he told himself fiercely, but she did not look like a woman going to an assignation. She looked more as if she were going to a wake.

Flora avoided the communal table at breakfast, even though she was now feeling hungry. She did not want to have to face him and his cruel barbs in front of others. She managed to beg a cup of coffee and take it to her room, with a couple of biscuits. It did not satisfy her hunger, but it served to stave off the worst pangs.

At eleven o'clock, they made their way down to the Brenta to board the *burchio.* Craythorne walked ahead with Catherine, Matthew walked with them, but kept casting an anxious eye backwards, and Mrs Wylde walked with Flora, tactfully refraining from asking what was wrong, but talking easily about commonplaces. Flora took in nothing of what was said, but Letty's voice had a soothing quality, and she found herself able to board the *burchio* with tolerable composure.

The journey was to take eight hours, and their host at the inn had had hampers packed for their refreshment during the journey. Lord Craythorne took Catherine to the bow of their barge and Flora went to the stern. From then on she remained there, not even moving from her seat when the rest of the party gathered together for refreshment.

'Come and have something to eat,' said Mrs Wylde. 'You have had next to nothing since yesterday, and it cannot be good for you.'

'No thank you, I . . . I am not hungry,' replied Flora.

'But my dear. . . .'

'Please leave me,' Flora insisted. 'I am not feeling well and shall be better on my own. You might. . . .' Here her voice nearly broke, but with an effort she managed to control it. 'You might keep an eye on Catherine for me, and . . . and send her my love.'

'Flora my dear, I have no way of knowing what has gone wrong, but will you allow me to intervene? I have known Leigh nearly all my life, and. . . .' Letty took another glance at her face and broke off. 'Very well, my dear,' she concluded. 'I hope you feel better soon. A sleep might do you good.' Flora leaned back in the comfortable seat and tried to sleep, but with indifferent success.

A short time later, her peace was again disturbed, this time by Matthew Warren. He was carrying a plate with some bread, chicken and fruit, and a glass of wine. He sat down next to her and said, 'Whatever has happened between you and Leigh, you aren't going to improve things by making yourself ill.' His kind words and practical advice caused the tears to start to her eyes again, but seeing the sense of what he said, she dried them quickly, took the food, and found that she was able to eat it and drink the wine. Matthew sat in silence watching her, and then said diffidently, 'I don't want to pry, and it's none of my business anyway, but if I can do anything to help, please tell me. The Lord knows you've done enough for me in your turn.'

'There's nothing,' she said in a subdued voice. 'Unless you can turn the clock back nine days.'

'Nine days! That's rather a tall order, but for you, Miss Chayter. . . .' He leaned forward, his hand on his heart. Despite her sombre mood, she could not help but smile. 'Nine days,' he went on in more normal tones. 'That would take us back to Milan – the day before we left. Now what happened then that has cut up your peace?' Flora looked at him in surprise. Behind his easy good nature he was obviously very acute.

'It's nothing,' she said agitatedly. 'It was just a manner of speech, that's all.' He bowed slightly, but Flora gained the impression that he did not believe her protestations. When she had finished the food and wine, he got up.

'I'll return later,' he said. As he walked back along the deck of the barge, Lord Craythorne approached him.

'Take care,' he said unsmilingly. 'You won't be the first man she's entrapped.'

'Entrapped?' said Matthew in a contemptuous tone that his cousin had never heard him use before. 'Don't be absurd, Leigh, it isn't in her nature.'

The earl laughed mirthlessly. 'It's at the very heart of her nature,' he replied, and made as if to walk away. Matthew caught him by the arm.

'Don't be a fool,' urged Matthew. 'Look, I've no idea what lies between you, but whatever it is, it's breaking her heart, that's for sure.'

Craythorne looked at him for a long moment, then said, 'Heart? She has no heart.'

'Leigh. . . .'

'Well, don't say I didn't warn you. I'd hate to see her hurt you, the way. . . .' He stopped abruptly and walked away, and this time Matthew did not detain him, but merely stared at his back, then towards the stern where Flora was sitting. Suddenly a lot of things were becoming clear.

They arrived in Venice as the sun was setting, and even Flora, feeling depressed as she did, could not help but feel her heart lift at the sight of the glowing sky touching the columns and towers of the city about which she had read so much.

Jane and her husband lived in the Palazzo Versace on the Grand Canal; it was to their home that they made their way immediately. The barge was tethered next to the mooring platform with the striped poles, and then it was time to disembark. There was no avoiding a meeting then. Flora had to approach the exit of the barge and, by ill-luck, reached it as Lord Craythorne did so from the opposite direction. He stepped aside to allow her to go first, and she nodded in acknowledgement of this courtesy. She was in a hurry to get out of his way quickly, and she stepped off the boat at the very moment when it was moving a little. This, coupled with the unaccustomed sensation of being on firm ground, and the fact that she had eaten very little that day, caused her to miss her footing and almost lose her balance, The earl, close behind, caught hold of her, and she was in his arms. All his cruelty was forgotten, as for a brief tantalizing moment she closed her eyes and drank in the sensation of being protected by his strength. Then with a murmur of thanks, she stepped away from him. She looked up at the *palazzo*, then the door opened and Jane flew across the threshold to greet them.

Chapter Thirteen

'Help you to find a new position? But Flora, why?' The greetings over, Jane had arranged that all her guests be conducted to their chambers. She was now quite heavily pregnant, so she contented herself with just taking her mother and Flora to their rooms and allowing her housekeeper to look after her other visitors. Naturally, mother and daughter had much to say to each other, but Flora guessed that Jane would come and see her as soon as possible, so she spent the time tidying herself up and getting ready to go down to dinner – a meal that she knew she would not be able to avoid without remark.

Quite soon, as she had anticipated, there was a gentle tap on the door and Jane came in, all smiles, which were quickly dispersed however, as soon as the first greetings were over.

'Jane, please can you help me to a new situation? Here in Venice, or with someone who is going back to England, it doesn't matter which.' Jane's puzzled exclamation was in response to this request.

'Surely you haven't quarrelled with Mama?' she went on in worried tones. Worry sat ill on Jane's placid features. Always a contented woman, marriage had given her a serenity which was very much a part of her.

'No, no indeed,' replied Flora. 'How could I possibly do so when she had been so kind?'

'With Craythorne, then.' Flora blushed. 'But surely it can be mended?'

'No, believe me, it cannot,' said Flora forcefully. 'Please, Jane, don't question me further.'

'Very well, I'll ask you no questions – for now. After all, dinner will soon be ready. And I will help you to find a new situation, if nothing else will do for you.' Here Flora hugged her, but then Jane held her at arms' length and said, 'But I must have the full story from you tomorrow, before I make any enquiries.'

Jane's husband, Roberto Versace, was an extremely handsome man in his late twenties, with a tanned complexion and sparkling eyes, and he was obviously delighted to be entertaining his wife's mother and friends under his roof. He was charming and courteous to all, but clearly his most tender care was reserved for his wife, and he was constantly glancing towards her to make sure that she was well and happy.

After a sumptuous meal, they made their way to a magnificent saloon decorated in red, with much gilding. As they entered the room, Jane caught her foot on the edge of the carpet and Roberto, ever watchful, moved swiftly to steady her. They settled down to talk, whilst Roberto rang for a servant, to whom he gave some whispered directions. Moments later, the servant returned and under Roberto's direction, proceeded to hammer some nails into the offending piece of carpet. Flora could not help but smile. Something about the tender way in which he looked after his wife tugged at her heart, and made her long for the same protective care. Aware of someone's eyes upon her, she looked across the room and saw Lord Craythorne returning her regard with an unreadable expression.

The following morning, Flora awoke to find that she had slept much later than she had intended. The emotional stress of the previous few days must have affected her physically more than she had realized at the time. A maid brought her chocolate and a pleasant kind of sweet bread, and after she had consumed this, she dressed and went downstairs to find out what was happening. She was anxious to avoid Craythorne, but judged that at this late hour, he would probably have left the house.

She was right. On going downstairs, she found Jane on her own sitting sewing, and the two women greeted one another warmly. Once Jane had ascertained that Flora had eaten, and wanted no more, she insisted that they sit down together.

'Roberto has gone to show Lord Craythorne and Mr Warren the sights, and Catherine has gone out with Mama and Cosette,' she said. 'So you see, you have no excuse now; you must tell me everything.'

Flora gave a deep sigh, then starting with Malcolm Brenner's arrival at The Lawns, she told Jane the whole story, only omitting the earl's kisses and his suggestion that she become his mistress. When she reached the end of the story, she turned to Jane and said, 'So you see, there is nothing for it but for me to leave and find a new post.'

'I see no such thing!' declared Jane indignantly. 'How could he possibly think so ill of you on such slim evidence, or refuse even to hear your account of events?'

'I don't know,' said Flora despairingly. 'But. . . .'

'Neither do I, and I think it is time somebody told him so!' So saying, she bit off her thread with extreme savagery, and picked up her scissors so determinedly that Flora could almost imagine her backing Craythorne up against the wall with them in her hand.

'Oh no, Jane, pray!' she cried. 'I have had quite enough of loud voices and accusations. Please! Or do you not think that you would be able to find me a place?'

'I am quite sure that I could,' replied Jane, putting her scissors back into her work bag, to Flora's great relief. 'Although in my opinion, you should not be the one who has to go. And besides, even though it might be a trifle awkward, you are not under any obligation to do as he tells you: you are, after all, not in his employ but in Mama's, and you are not his guest but mine. You have only been looking after Catherine to oblige him. Now that you are here in Venice, he will be able to hire someone else to care for Catherine – if she needs anyone beside Cosette, who seems to be very capable. The *palazzo* is large; you need hardly meet; you are both civilized people.'

'No,' said Flora despairingly. 'I cannot . . . I just cannot. . . .' Her voice died away.

'Flora, there is something you have not told me, isn't there?'

There was another long silence, then Flora said bitterly, 'He asked me to become his mistress.'

'Flora, no!' cried Jane in shocked tones. 'Well that settles it! The man is quite without sense or sensitivity, not to mention being too dense to work out what is just under his nose. Mama has always brought me up to believe him to be a man of honour, but. . . .'

'He believes me to have no morals,' interrupted Flora, driven by a need to defend him. 'He could hardly make any other sort of proposal, could he?' Suddenly aware that she might have given away too much, she blushed and looked away.

'And you would have another sort, is that it?' asked Jane acutely. Then a moment or two later, she added, 'Flora, are you in love with him?'

Flora darted one more glance at her, then rose to her feet and walked to the window. The Grand Canal was now, at eleven o'clock, a-bustle with life.

'You see, it's quite hopeless,' she said, carefully avoiding answering the question. 'Another situation is the only thing that will fit the bill.'

'Well, we shall see,' said Jane, wisely refraining from probing any further. 'For the time being, things must remain as they are. A too sudden departure after your arrival could easily encourage the very scandal that you are most anxious to avoid. In these early days, you will be out and about all the time. There will be very little need to see him at all.'

'That was what Aunt Letty said in Calais,' said Flora darkly.

It nearly broke Flora's heart to miss so much of Venice, but she was determined to avoid the earl. He spent much of the time out and about, so therefore Flora spent much of her time inside. Jane, at first inclined to protest, soon accepted Flora's companionship gratefully, and the two women found themselves renewing a much-valued friendship. Sometimes, Mrs Wylde stayed with them, and then the conversation was a three way one, ranging gently around the sewing or drawing that each might be doing, or the activities of Venetians, or household interests, but almost never touching Lord Craythorne. If ever Letty seemed about to refer to him, her daughter had but to mention the coming baby and the grandmother-to-be was easily diverted.

Signor Versace also spent as much time at home as he could spare – for he was a man with many claims upon his time – and it was inevitable that he and Flora should get to know one another quite well. Flora, who had not had the chance to meet him more than twice before his marriage to Jane, found herself understanding why her friend should have fallen in love with this handsome, kindly gentleman. For his part, Roberto soon came to regard Flora highly as he saw how much good her presence did for Jane's spirits, which had begun to droop a little as advanced pregnancy made her more uncomfortable.

It was inevitable that Flora and Craythorne should meet in the evenings, but when necessity demanded conversation between them, they both confined their remarks to commonplaces. Flora still felt angry when she thought about the assumptions he had made about her, but her anger had now cooled to dull despair. Never were the earl's smiles turned towards her now; they were kept for almost any other member of the human race.

One evening as they were sitting after dinner, Flora looked up to see Craythorne bending over a book with Catherine, pointing something out to her. The girl looked up at him and they smiled into each other's eyes. The moment caught Flora off guard, and she was suddenly tempted afresh by the earl's disgraceful offer. She felt such a wave of longing that she closed her eyes in order to regain her composure.

'*Signorina*, are you quite well?' asked Roberto. She opened her eyes and found that he was bending over her with an expression of anxious concern on his face. She had started a little at his words, for she had not supposed anyone to be so near to her.

She smiled rather uncertainly and said, 'I am well; a little tired, perhaps.'

'Not so much tired as lacking in fresh air, I think,' he answered her. 'You never go out, *signorina*! Do not think that I am not grateful for your care for my Jane. But this is your first visit to Venice. Tomorrow you will go out. I insist upon it!' She smiled again at his kindness, then glanced over at Lord Craythorne. He had stopped what he was doing and was staring at them, an expression of fury on his face. Suddenly, Flora could not bear to be under his disapproving eye any longer.

'Perhaps I had better retire now,' she said to her host as she rose. 'Pray say my "goodnights" for me.'

'Very well,' he replied. Then he added in a conspiratorial tone, 'but do not think that I will forget about my little suggestion!' Flora curtsied and turned to go, to find the earl standing close behind her. All at once she remembered her thoughts as she had looked at him from across the room, and she blushed.

'Allow me to get you a candle, ma'am,' were his innocuous words, but his expression promised something far more threatening. When they reached the bottom of the dark stairs,

Craythorne said to her, 'You never cease to astound me. Just when I think that you have reached the nadir of contemptibility, you find new depths with which to confront me.'

'Indeed, My Lord,' replied Flora, her heart beating fast. 'And you are for ever astounding me with the vividness of your imagination. With what villainy are you crediting me now? Why, I have scarcely left the *palazzo*!'

'Precisely, ma'am,' he replied. She stared at him for a long moment, before comprehension began to dawn in her eyes.

'Oh no,' she whispered, her face now as white as it had been red earlier on.

'Yes, and don't pretend innocence to me. I've caught you out in that game before, remember?'

'Game? What game?'

'Any man will do with you, won't he? Any man except me, apparently. Not even your friend's husband is safe. Have you no sense of honour, no decency?'

'How can you believe me to be so base?' she asked in shocked tones. 'Signor Versace has been kind to me.'

'Signor Versace!' sneered the earl. 'Is that what you call him in bed?' Unable to bear any more of his slanders, Flora lifted her hand, and dashed the candle that he held to the floor. Then, picking up her skirts, she ran up the dark stairs, aiming for the sanctuary of her room. For a few moments, she could only hear the sound of her own movements, then behind her, like some character from a nightmare, she heard his feet thundering up the stairs two at a time. He reached her just as she had got to her chamber, and seizing hold of her, he pushed her against the door and seemed about to kiss her. Suddenly, Flora could not bear the thought of another loveless embrace, and she turned her face aside. His strength was so much greater than hers that he could easily have forced her, but instead, he released her and stepped back, saying in tones that spoke as much of despair as anger, 'Tell me – why not me?' She looked straight at him, her only desire at that moment to hurt him as he had hurt her.

'Because I find you so utterly disgusting that I would sooner drown myself in the canal than endure your slightest touch.' So saying, she felt behind her for the door handle, opened the door and entered her chamber. He made no attempt to stop her. Once inside, she leaned against the door and listened hard. After a few moments, she heard the sound of his footsteps as he walked away.

Chapter Fourteen

The following morning, Flora went to Jane, and insisted that she could not possibly stay any longer. If Jane noticed a degree of panic in her demeanour, she did not mention it, but she was able to give Flora some welcome news.

'I have had a note this very morning from an acquaintance who knows of a couple who wish to travel back to England almost immediately,' she said. 'They are a respectable couple, but the wife is rather sickly, so the husband is anxious to find a companion for her who will be able to care for her and take her mind off the rigours of the journey.' For a moment, Flora mentally contrasted the companionable time that she had spent on the way to Venice with the possible drudgery of the return journey, but then she remembered how urgent was the need for departure.

'I will take the position,' she said. 'Will you please write and secure it for me straight away?'

Jane sighed. 'I thought that that was what you might say,' she answered. 'Oh Flora, are you certain that this is what you want?'

Flora smiled bitterly. 'It is not what I want at all,' she replied, in measured tones. 'But it is the only honourable course open to me.' Then as if she could not help herself she said, 'Why is he so determined to think ill of me? I have made one stupid blunder; just one; and it appears that I am to pay for it over and over again.' There was no need for Jane to ask to whom she was referring.

Later on that morning, Jane received a reply to her note, and she took it up to Flora's room.

'It appears that these people – Mr and Mrs Proudfoot – will take you as soon as you can come to them,' she said. 'They are staying at the Leon Bianco, so they must be well-to-do.'

'Then I had better hurry if I am to join them today,' said Flora, taking one of her bags from a chest where it had been stored in order to start packing.

'Today!' cried Jane. 'Oh no! But I had hoped that you would stay with us until the last minute – or at least for a farewell dinner.'

'No, thank you,' said Flora, tight-lipped. 'I must go as soon as I have packed.'

'Oh dear,' exclaimed Jane wringing her hands. 'If only I had told you that they wanted to see you tomorrow!'

Flora laughed. 'You could not possibly be so devious,' she said.

'Then at least allow me to pack your things and have them sent to the Leon Bianco,' insisted Jane. 'I will not have you arriving there with all your baggage, for all the world as if you had been thrown out.' This Flora agreed to, taking only what she would need for overnight in a small bag. 'Now promise me that you will not leave without seeing me again,' added her hostess.

'Very well,' agreed Flora. 'I will visit you before I leave Venice.' She turned to check the items that she was going to put in her overnight bag.

While she was looking down, Jane said softly, 'He must have hurt you dreadfully.'

'Yes, perhaps, but it's all over now,' replied Flora, without looking up.

The news of Flora's departure was greeted with different reactions by all the members of the party. Catherine was disappointed and surprised that Flora had not said goodbye to her, and was inclined to blame herself.

'Oh Mrs Versace, are you quite sure that it is not because of anything that I have done?' she asked anxiously.

'Certainly not, my dear,' said Jane decisively. 'You have nothing with which to reproach yourself,' she added, looking rather pointedly at Lord Craythorne.

'I am rather surprised that she did not say goodbye,' said Mrs Wylde in puzzled tones.

'She needed to take the place immediately, or lose it,' Jane explained. 'She was particularly concerned not to offend you, Mama, as you have been employing her, and as you have been so kind.'

'As to that, I never thought of our relationship in those terms,' answered her mother. 'But if as you say, she is to return and bid us all farewell, then I shall be glad to have a chance to see her again. It is perhaps no bad thing for you to have one less guest in your condition, my dear.'

'Flora seemed so happy with us earlier on,' remarked Matthew Warren, looking pointedly at his cousin. 'I wonder what – or who – upset her?'

Craythorne had been standing with his back to the assembled company. Now he turned, his expression impassive, and said, 'She is a grown woman. She is surely entitled to do as she pleases.'

Jane, unable to remain silent in the face of this, looked straight at him and said, 'It did not please her at all, but she could find no honourable alternative.' He said nothing, but simply stared at her for a long moment.

After the meal was over, Matthew begged the favour of a private interview with his cousin. Roberto Versace offered the use of his library for the purpose and when the door had closed, Craythorne turned to his favourite cousin.

'Well, Matthew, in what way may I serve you?'

'I have not come to ask for any favours,' said Matthew, his head held high. He had always held his exalted cousin in considerable esteem, but his perception of Craythorne's treatment of Flora had rocked him considerably. 'I simply want to inform you of my intention to marry.' Craythorne paused in the act of pouring the brandy which Roberto had provided for his guests' use and stared at his kinsman.

'Indeed,' he replied eventually. 'Then I am bound to tell you that I think you are making a mistake.'

'Really?' said Matthew with a hauteur that his cousin had not experienced from him before. 'And in what area do you think my error might lie?'

Craythorne looked at him for a long moment before saying, 'I beg your pardon. You remind me, very properly, that you are of an age to make your own decisions. Your position in my employ, and that of your mother in my care, will remain unchanged, of course.'

'I'm obliged to you,' said Matthew bowing stiffly. He turned to go, but the earl halted him.

'One moment, Matthew. I may not dictate to you, nor would I wish to do so, but as the head of the family I am entitled to advise, and in that capacity I must implore you to consider whether you have given sufficient thought to the step that you are taking.'

'I believe I have,' said Matthew, his chin high. Any onlooker would have said then that he had never before looked more like his formidable cousin than at that moment.

'Marriage is a serious business. I would not have you discover later that you had regrets.'

'First you talk of mistakes; now regrets. Tell me, Cousin, what exactly do you hold against my future wife? Is it your intention to blacken her character? Or is her station simply not exalted enough for your tastes?' Craythorne put down his brandy glass with a snap.

'Her station in life is a matter of indifference to me,' he retorted. 'But you force me to say that her character is quite another matter. It is not my intention to blacken anyone's name, but frankly she has not behaved as a lady should.' Matthew, too, put down his brandy glass so violently that liquid slopped over the side.

'Devil take me, Leigh, but you'll not speak of her this way!'

'Matthew, I make every allowance for your infatuation. . . .'

'Infatuation! I—'

'Yes, infatuation, but you must allow that I have something to say! After all, I have known her for longer than you have, and—'

'What the deuce do you mean by that?' demanded Matthew. 'We all met her for the first time in Paris!'

'Paris?' queried the earl. 'Matthew, what are you talking about?'

'Are you foxed?' asked Matthew, as puzzled now as his kinsman. 'We are talking about my marriage – to Cosette.'

'Cosette?' murmured His Lordship.

'Of course, Cosette. Now – do I have your consent?' Craythorne stared at him, then gave a short laugh and shook his head as if to clear it.

'Of course I wish you joy,' he said. 'I had no idea that your interests lay in that direction, and I have far too much respect for my own skin to enquire any further.' After looking at him a little warily, Matthew took the hand that he was holding out and shook it. 'Now, shall we finish our brandy?' went on the earl.

After the two men had drunk in silence, Matthew said slowly, 'If you were not concerned about Cosette's character and background, then who did you think I was intending to marry?'

'Why, Miss Chayter of course,' answered the earl, looking

down into his brandy. 'You cannot deny, I think, that there was something between you at one time; although I am very glad that you escaped that particular trap.'

'No indeed, on my honour,' declared Matthew, somewhat mystified. 'Oh, I suppose I flirted a little with her in Paris, but she didn't like it above half. She was much happier when we were just friends.'

'Really,' said the earl drily.

'Oh yes. In fact, she was very sympathetic when I told her of my feelings for Cosette. She promised to help if she could. In fact,' he grinned, 'she even diverted you from us on one occasion.' Craythorne looked puzzled, and signalled for him to go on. 'At the inn at Turin, in the garden. I was meeting Cosette, and Flora came to fetch us in.'

'Miss Chayter was not meeting you herself?'

'Certainly not. In fact, she did not like the role she was playing above half. She insisted that you should be told about our attachment as soon as possible. Flora's a splendid girl, but not the one for me.' When Leigh said nothing, Matthew went on, 'She was very concerned about your feelings. I wonder, Leigh, whether you should have been more concerned about hers?' He drained the last of his brandy and quietly left the room. Lord Craythorne remained there for some considerable time, lost in thought.

Mr and Mrs Proudfoot proved to be a kindly, undemanding couple, but Flora could not help but think that her time with them would prove to be rather dull. Mr Proudfoot was a very quiet man with very little conversation beyond the absolute necessities. Mrs Proudfoot talked endlessly and in great detail about her children, her needlework and her illnesses, and she displayed a reassuring lack of curiosity concerning Flora's background and reasons for returning to England so soon after her arrival.

Of one thing she had cause to be thankful. At least, she would now be certain of a reference from the Proudfoots when they reached England, and hopefully she would be able to find a situation as far away from Craythorne and any of his residences as possible.

The Leon Bianco was situated on the Grand Canal, with a fine view of the Rialto to one side. Whilst Mrs Proudfoot slept in the afternoon, after being read to, Flora wandered on to the balcony to look at the scene below. There were gondolas darting to and fro, people in them looking relaxed and happy. How she wished that she could have enjoyed Venice in that same frame of mind!

At one point a gondola came past with a gentleman as its passenger, a man with black curly hair, and for a moment she wondered whether it might be Craythorne. Then he looked up and saw her, and she realized that it was not the earl. The young man, seeing a pretty girl watching him, drew his own conclusions and blew her a kiss. She had to smile; but the extent to which her heart had leapt at first sight of him, and then sunk at the revelation of his features, told its own story. Her head told her heart that she was a fool, but her treacherous heart would not listen to reason. Away from him, it was easy to forget the harsh things that he had said, and just to remember that she loved him and missed him.

The day before the Proudfoots were due to leave Venice, Flora set off to go back to the Palazzo Versace to say goodbye to Jane as she had promised. She walked there, enjoying the sights and sounds of the city, and trying to remember as much as possible. She would never be able to afford another visit to Venice, that was certain.

Suddenly taking in the implications of this, she decided to visit St Mark's Square just once. Mrs Proudfoot was resting and had told her to take her time. It seemed very unfair that she should completely miss one of Venice's greatest marvels.

She stood for a time in the square admiring the entrance to the famous church, then wandered over to the two great pillars that framed the view of the lagoon. It was so beautiful that she found herself longing for someone with whom to share it, but not for just anyone – for a special person. She moved closer to the water, imagining the Doge leaving the Basilica to her left in his ceremonial barge and sailing out in order to wed the sea in the ancient ceremony that signified the dependency of Venice upon the water that was so much a part of it. Then, recalling that she had intended to visit St Mark's and that she must leave enough time for Jane, she turned around to go back. Standing a short distance away from her and blocking the way in which she had intended to go was Lord Craythorne. He was watching her, his face impassive, his black hair stirring gently about his shoulders.

'Miss Chayter. Have you been to the *palazzo*?' he asked her. She stood looking at him as if he was an apparition. 'I have been talking to Matthew. He has told me. . . . Miss Chayter, I. . . .'

She did not take in what he was saying. She had already said goodbye to him in her heart. The last thing that she wanted was to hear more hurtful things from him, and she was convinced that that was all he would have to say to her.

'No,' she said, shaking her head and backing away, her hands over her ears. 'No, I won't listen! I can't bear it any more!'

He stepped towards her then, saying urgently, 'Flora be careful! The canal!' She barely heard his words and did not take in what he was saying, but took two more steps back until she found herself stepping into fresh air, then the sky turned topsy-turvy, there was a rush of water, something struck her on the head and she knew no more.

Chapter Fifteen

Jane had been expecting Flora to arrive, but not in the manner in which she did so that afternoon, in a gondola, dripping wet and unconscious, and carried to the door by a similarly soaking Lord Craythorne, who said, 'She fell in the canal and struck her head. Send for the doctor as fast as you can.'

Flora's room had been cleaned and the bed made, and it was to this room that the earl carried her, his face white and set. Not until he was certain that there were enough people to care for her did he leave the room to take off his wet things. The water had not been pleasant smelling and he was glad to discover that a bath was being prepared for him. Roberto's own valet had been sent to attend him, and he was just dressing in clean clothes with that worthy's assistance when there was a knock on the door of his chamber. The valet opened the door to admit the doctor, whom Jane had sent to attend the earl after he had examined Flora. The doctor applauded the fact that Craythorne had immediately bathed and then enquired whether he had swallowed any of the water. The earl shook his head.

'No, I took a deep breath as I dived in and got her out as quickly as possible. There were plenty of people on the canal side to help us out.'

'Then I can be optimistic about your recovery,' said the

doctor. 'As to the young lady. . . .' He shook his head, his expression grave. Craythorne stiffened.

'What do you mean?' he asked sharply. 'I got her out quickly enough. She struck her head, I know, but she was certainly breathing.'

'*Signor*, the water in Venice may look beautiful, but it is not clean. Surely you must have noticed the smell on your own clothes after you came out? There may be poisons that she has swallowed, and if so. . . .' He made a little fatalistic gesture with his hands. The earl, still only in breeches and shirt, made as if to seize hold of the doctor's coat with his hands, then recollected himself and murmured an apology.

'Tell me, will she . . . die?' The doctor, more accustomed to extravagant gestures than his English colleagues, and drawing his own conclusions about the reasons for this nobleman's concern, took this in his stride.

'*Signor*, I cannot tell, but she is receiving the best of care and she is in God's hands. I will do all I can, I assure you.'

After the doctor had gone, Craythorne stood for a long time without moving. In a way that was most unlike him, he allowed Roberto's valet to finish fastening his shirt, tie his cravat, and ease on his waistcoat. Then, suddenly, he pulled himself together.

'Thank you, Tonio, I can manage now,' he said. The valet bowed and left closing the door behind him.

If Craythorne could have avoided meeting the others that evening, he would have done so, for his thoughts were in considerable turmoil. For days now, he had been whipping himself into a fury at the thought of Flora's perfidy. The news that Matthew was to marry Cosette, and that Flora had merely been helping them, not meeting Matthew herself, had given him pause for thought. He had wanted to speak to Flora when he had seen her that afternoon, not knowing what to say, but knowing that he could not bear to let her go. Now, the news that she might not survive had rocked him on his heels. He was accustomed to being in control of what was going on. Now, it seemed that Flora might die, and he would not be able to do a thing to prevent it. Unable to bear the direction in which his thoughts were taking him, he made his way downstairs.

It was a very subdued party who gathered for dinner that night. Catherine, for once, was dining in the nursery with Cosette. It was judged that the atmosphere of anxiety, coupled with the inevitable speculation about Flora's health, would be too distressing for her. Jane did not come downstairs, as she was eating from a tray in Flora's room, and consequently Roberto although courteous, was rather distracted. Matthew was stiffly polite, but also gave the impression of one who had much to say but knew that this was neither the time nor the place. Mrs Wylde tried to maintain a flow of commonplaces with less than complete success. Craythorne said nothing, and ate little more. No one did justice to the excellent meal set before them; and afterwards, no one showed any disposition to linger. Roberto, with a murmured excuse, went to see how Jane was faring; Mrs Wylde retired to her chamber; Matthew, after a long stare at his cousin, left the room without so much as an apology; and Craythorne was left with the distinct impression that he was nobody's friend.

He went up to his room, paused with his hand on the door handle, then walked to Flora's room instead, opened the door and went inside. There was no sign of Jane. Flora lay in bed with the covers pulled up to her chin, her fluffy blonde hair clustered about her pale face. She was so still, that for a horrible moment he thought that she might be dead, and he strode hastily towards the bed. To his relief he could see the counterpane gently rising and falling with her breathing. He closed his eyes, and found himself praying. After a few moments, feeling a little calmer, he opened them again, and hearing a movement behind him, he turned to look round. Jane was standing on the threshold. She had obviously been crying.

'Haven't you done enough?' she asked him. 'Was it not sufficient for you to drive her from this house without trying to drown her as well?' Here in Flora's chamber with her lifeless-seeming body in their very presence, he felt like a murderer.

'I didn't mean to hurt her, I swear,' he said defensively.

'Oh really,' replied Jane stonily. 'Just as you did not mean to ask her to be your mistress or treat her with such appalling coldness and contempt.'

'Signora Versace, I appreciate that she is your friend; I also appreciate that you are distressed. But I have to tell you that her conduct was not what that of a lady should be.'

'One mistake,' said Jane, her voice unsteady. 'She made one mistake, and for that you have made her pay and pay and pay again.'

'There have been others,' he murmured uncertainly. Jane took a deep breath.

'Lord Craythorne, I have known Flora for almost all her life. I know her heart. She is good and honourable and true. Whatever you may have seen or heard, she is blameless, I assure you.'

'How can you be so certain of that when you were not there?' he asked her quietly.

'Why are you so determined to think badly of her?' she countered. He turned away.

'The evidence . . .' he began.

'What evidence? I think that if you examine your evidence carefully, My Lord, you may find that it exists only in your own mind.' She gave him time to let that sink in, then added, 'Why do you hate her so much?'

'I? Hate her?' he asked incredulously.

'She certainly thinks so, whereas she, poor girl. . . .' She stopped, aware that she was on the point of betraying Flora's confidence.

'Well, ma'am?' prompted the earl, conscious that something very important was about to be disclosed.

'I cannot tell you what she said, sir,' said Jane with simple dignity. 'But suffice it to say that if you knew her heart, you would understand that there is one overwhelming reason why she could never have behaved in the way of which you accuse her.' At that moment, Flora stirred slightly. 'I have promised Roberto that I will retire immediately,' she said. 'Contrary to your suspicions, My Lord, Roberto has no interest in any other woman than myself. And no, before you ask, Flora did not tell me: I could see it in your face. Your imagination does you little honour. Excuse me, I must come and ring for the maid to sit with her.'

'No,' said the earl. 'You are right in saying that I have much to think about. I will stay with her. Just give me a few moments to change.' He walked slowly back to his room and once inside, removed his evening coat of plum brocade. He was on the point of taking off his cravat, when there was a perfunctory knock on the door, and Matthew walked in.

'Well, are you satisfied now?' said Matthew angrily. 'Now that you have driven her to her death?' It was almost exactly what Jane had said just a few minutes before. Craythorne took a step back, and turned deathly pale again.

'Matthew, she is not. . . ?'

'No! But no thanks to you! You make me sick. Everyone's calling you a hero because you rescued her from the water. She wouldn't even have been there if you hadn't driven her out of this house. What other vicious slanders did you throw at her before she left the *palazzo*?'

'None, upon my honour!'

'Honour! That's rich!' Matthew spat out. 'All my life I've admired you, looked up to you, almost like a father, because of your honour! What kind of honour slanders an innocent young woman in the way that you have done? And another thing: what was it that made her fall in?'

'Matthew, I. . . .'

'If you ask me, she saw you, and she was so frightened that she—'

'Stop!' said Craythorne in a voice that was not quite steady. 'Do you think you can possibly say anything to me that I have not told myself twenty times already? Do you think I don't blame myself for what happened?' He turned away, walked to the fireplace, grasped hold of the mantelpiece with both hands and bowed his head. They were both silent for a time, then the earl went on, 'The last time I saw her, she told me that she would rather throw herself in the canal than have me touch her.' He turned to face his cousin, his face a mask of anguish. 'I never thought she meant it.'

Shortly afterwards, Craythorne returned to Flora's room where Jane was still waiting.

'She has not stirred,' she said. She was silent whilst they both looked at the still figure of Flora Chayter.

'You must go,' the earl said at last. 'You need your rest.' Jane walked towards the door, then came back and impulsively squeezed his hand.

'I shall pray for you both,' she said. After she had gone, Craythorne sat down, his eyes fixed on the occupant of the bed. He remained thus for a long time, lost in thought.

It was later that night that Flora regained consciousness. The earl had thought that any increase in animation would bring him inexpressible relief, but the change that occurred was scarcely such as to cheer him, for she seemed delirious, unable to recognize him, and complained that her head hurt her. He tried to organize her pillows in a more comfortable arrangement, but no sooner had he done so than she was overcome with the most distressing sickness, for which the earl was at first completely unprepared. He hurried to get the washing basin as quickly as he could, and when the first spasm had abated, he rang for someone to come and change the linen. Alerted by the disturbance, Mrs Wylde came, wanting to help, but the sight of someone acutely nauseous had the effect of making her feel ill herself.

'Send for Cosette,' said the earl. 'You can best help by going to stay with Catherine in her place.' The Frenchwoman came and, as Craythorne had hoped, she was totally unflustered by the whole business. She was soon bustling about organizing the maids of the *palazzo*, getting the bed stripped, ordering clean linen and fresh nightwear for Flora, and plenty of old sheets and rags, for the bed was bound to be soiled again. Craythorne, meanwhile, was supporting Flora in his arms, heedless of the damage to his own clothes, and keeping the basin nearby in case of need.

'I can manage now, *Milor*',' said Cosette, when everything was in order again.

'I'm staying,' answered the earl. Among other things, Cosette had arranged for a truckle bed to be set up in the room behind a screen.

'Then you sleep,' said Cosette, pointing to the screen. When Craythorne started to protest, Cosette, who seemed to have no idea of her proper place, said, '*Milor*', I am right in this. I have already slept, and you have not. I will wake you later. We will take turns. Now give me your shirt and I will send for a new one.'

'You're a sensible woman,' he answered as he unbuttoned his shirt. 'Very well, but don't forget to wake me.' As he took it off and handed it to her, he encountered a decidedly measuring look from her, as she eyed his naked chest. He raised one eyebrow, and said pointedly, 'I believe I am to wish you joy on your engagement to Matthew.'

Cosette looked down modestly, and said, with a polite curtsy, 'Thank you, *Milor*'. I love Matthew with all my heart, and will be faithful to him But,' she added mischievously before whisking out of the door with his shirt, 'a girl can look!' He could not help but grin at her impudence, but it occurred to him that never had he seen Flora look at a man in the way that Cosette had just looked at him.

He lay down on the truckle bed, but it didn't proved necessary for Cosette to wake him throughout the whole of that long, dark night. Every time the distressing sounds of retching were heard, he was out of his bed, ready to support Flora and aid Cosette in all that needed to be done. He thought that he had never spent such a long night in his life before. With each bout of sickness, Flora seemed to become weaker.

It appeared that no one in the household had been able to sleep successfully, for towards dawn, Roberto came to the room to ask if there was anything he could do.

'I think that we must send for the doctor again,' said Craythorne. His eyes were red-rimmed, his face pale, his chin unshaven.

'It is already done,' replied Roberto. He, too, looked as if he had slept little.

'Then I don't know what else we can do,' said Craythorne helplessly. 'We lift her, we support her, we watch her go through agonies, we clean her up, and all the time she gets weaker and weaker.'

'Has she taken anything?' asked Roberto. This whole conversation was taking place on the threshold in hushed voices.

'She keeps nothing down,' answered the earl. 'Perhaps something to drink might refresh her; give her another taste in her mouth.'

Roberto nodded. 'Your Flora, she has been such an angel to my Jane, that I want to do all I can for her.' He looked directly at the earl. 'Anyone can make a mistaken judgement about someone, *signor*: the secret is to be prepared to acknowledge that mistake.'

Shortly afterwards, the housekeeper herself came upstairs with something in a jug.

'It is a drink made with herbs,' she said. 'My nephew fell into the canal when he was small and this recipe helped him.' Craythorne gave Flora some of the drink, which she took thirstily, and it seemed to give her a measure of relief. Although she brought back most of it later, at least it appeared to spare her that dreadful dry retching.

The doctor arrived shortly afterwards, and he could only shake his head and say that it was just as he had feared. He was glad that Craythorne was not similarly afflicted, and shrugged at the idea of the herb drink.

'It will not harm her, and may do some good,' he said. 'There is no telling what may be the value of these old family remedies.' He offered to call again, which offer the earl accepted, but later, Cosette (who had made no serious attempts to flirt with him) said, 'You and me, *Milor*', we make as good a doctor as he.'

Throughout that day, and the first part of the next night, Flora continued to take the herbal drink, and later to bring it back, but as time went by, the sickness diminished, until eventually it ceased altogether. Craythorne was thankful that she now appeared to be at peace, but she was so pale and still that he was afraid that even now, she might slip away from them. Although it was his turn to watch, he was so tired, for he had hardly slept at all the previous night, that he fell asleep in his chair, which was set beside the bed.

Waking in an awkward position in the grey light of dawn, he flexed his neck and shoulders, then looked across at the bed. The counterpane did not appear to be moving. His heart gave a lurch, and suddenly he fully realized what it would mean to him to lose her. Hardly daring to hope, he leaned forward to discover whether she was breathing. When he felt her breath on his cheek, his feeling of relief was so intense that for a moment he was incapable of any movement at all, or any other thought than thankfulness to God that she was alive. Then, drawing back a little, he noticed that the pillow on which she was resting had become very crumpled. Carefully lifting her against him, he turned the pillow and laid her gently down again, but as he let go of her, one frail hand crept unsteadily up to his cheek, and brushed against it with trembling fingers. For a moment, hard grey eyes looked down into blue ones, and she murmured drowsily, 'Exactly like a pirate,' before drifting off once more into a doze.

When Cosette awoke and came to take her turn at Flora's bedside, she found the earl asleep in his chair, but this time, he was holding the sleeping girl's left hand in his right.

From then onwards, Flora made a steady if slow recovery. Mr and Mrs Proudfoot sent their sympathy and regrets, but had felt bound to employ another companion, as their need to return to England was urgent. Now that Flora no longer needed nursing care, Mrs Wylde and Jane were both able to take a turn in the sickroom, giving the earl and Cosette some much needed rest. Craythorne also took the opportunity of walking outside. It was the first time that he had been out of the house since he had returned with Flora in his arms.

It was as he was coming back to the *palazzo* that he met Matthew Warren, who was just coming to find him. Although Matthew had played no part in nursing Flora, he had proved invaluable in diverting Catherine and escorting her and Mrs Wylde about the city. The two cousins had not spoken beyond simple enquiries as to Flora's health and Catherine's whereabouts since the harsh words that they had exchanged after the accident. Now, confronted with one another, they stood in silence for a moment, and when each man put out his hand, it would have been hard to say who was the first to do so.

'Leigh, I said some harsh things to you,' said Matthew.

'Things that should never have been said. I want to ask your pardon for. . . .'

'No, Matthew,' replied Craythorne. 'You said nothing that was not deserved. Your father was a gallant gentleman, and he would have been proud of you.'

'Leigh—' The earl held up his hand.

'The only thing I find it hard to forgive is the idea that you look upon me as a father! My dear fellow, you are twenty-four, and I am thirty-seven. I do not recall being that precocious at thirteen!' They laughed, both relieved at the mending of a relationship which meant a great deal to both of them. Together, they went inside and entered one of the *palazzo*'s many reception rooms, where they were served with wine.

'Leigh, I received a letter this morning,' said Matthew, after the wine had been tasted and approved. 'It is from Malcolm, and in it he speaks about Flora.' Leigh turned towards him, his face set, his hand raised in a warning gesture.

'I hope you don't intend to take his part,' he said warningly. 'He has done his damnedest to ruin her life, and because of my blind stupidity, I almost allowed him to succeed. Well, never again, I swear it.'

'Well, here's a turnaround!' exclaimed his cousin. Craythorne flushed.

'I've had time to think,' he said, looking down into his glass. 'Ever since Padua – Milan really – some kind of madness has had me in its grip. It's as if I've been seeing everything through a red mist. But when she sank beneath the waters, it was as if that mist was dispersed; and later, as I nursed her and held her in my arms, I realized what a fool I had been, and what was really important to me.' He looked up at Matthew. 'It isn't Malcolm and his whinings, that's for sure.'

'Then you are in love with her,' said Matthew. 'I thought as much when you were so angry with her at Padua.'

The earl smiled ruefully. 'You are wiser than I, for although

I suppose I have known it for a long time, I did not really acknowledge my feelings for her until I thought I might lose her.'

'So when am I to wish you joy?' asked Matthew tentatively.

'After all the things I've said to her?' replied Craythorne with wry bitterness. 'The best I can hope for is that I shall be forgiven.'

In the silence that followed, Matthew refilled both their glasses. Then at last he said, 'Let me tell you about Malcolm. There's nothing in his letter to Flora's detriment – quite the contrary, in fact – and it might divert you.' Craythorne gestured for him to continue and they both sat down. Matthew took the letter out of his coat. 'The first part of this enthralling letter is concerned with the charms of Marietta his wife, and with how I have always been his favourite cousin, being . . . where are we? Ah yes; "a first rate fellow and always ready to give a friend assistance whenever possible". Having charmed me with that, he proceeds to tell me about his wedding – at which, I gather, he cut a gallant and handsome figure, with his bride the most beautiful woman who ever graced the earth, whereas you, My Lord, "glowered in the background like a bird of ill-omen" – I rather like that, Leigh, don't you?' Despite himself, Craythorne was beginning to grin.

'I certainly felt a little like one,' he admitted. 'Go on, Matthew, I believe I can guess where we're getting to – although perchance I misjudge the lad.'

'Not at all,' answered Matthew. 'Now Marietta, being so charming, delightful, beautiful etc., is worthy of having a considerable sum of money lavished upon her, which Malcolm, sadly enough, does not have. Of course, Marietta has plenty, but delicacy forbids him from bestowing gifts upon her that have been purchased with her own money. . . .'

'In other words, her family won't give him any; very wise of them!'

'. . . and you have proved yourself to be too mean to give him any, so he is applying to me – as if I have the means to pay for his drinking and gaming, for that is what it amounts to! Then he says this: "I met Flora by chance in the Duomo at Milan. . . ." '

'Flora? Damn his impudence,' growled the earl, his smiles vanishing, his brows drawing together.

' " . . . and she refused to try to get any money out of Craythorne for me, so I must reluctantly apply to you". He signs himself "your affectionate Cousin". Affectionate, my eye!'

'May I see the letter?' asked the earl. Matthew put the paper into his outstretched hand. ' "By chance"! I spoke to him in Milan. He gave me the impression, without exactly saying so, that Flora had agreed to an assignation.' He thought for a moment, an expression of deep regret on his face. 'Matthew, she tried to tell me the truth, but I would not listen. How can I ever expect her to forgive me now?'

'Perhaps the answer is not to expect it, but to ask for it humbly,' suggested Matthew tentatively. It was not often that his formidable cousin asked for his advice. 'She may be more willing to listen to you than you suppose.'

'Let us certainly hope that she is more willing to listen than I deserve,' agreed the earl. 'But to get back to Malcolm: did he really think that you would not share this letter with me?'

'He has no understanding of a relationship in which people do not make use of each other,' replied Matthew. 'In that respect, he is to be pitied. Was it to arrange his marriage that you stayed behind in Milan?'

Craythorne nodded. 'It would have been useful to have been able to puff my consequence up a little more. Having only a groom and horse and enough clothing for a change, I looked like an adventurer myself! Luckily, an acquaintance of Marietta's family had been to London recently, and was able to assure them of my probity and respectability.'

'And the delectable Marietta?'

'Oh, a diamond, undoubtedly, although my taste runs more to fair women.' (At this point, Matthew raised his glass to his cousin in a silent toast, which the earl acknowledged with a slight bow.) 'She is charming too, but I fancy with a hint of steel which I don't think Malcolm suspects as yet. She also has three brothers, one heir to the estate, one in the army, and the third the most formidable priest I've ever met in my life. The marriage was certainly what Malcolm desired, but he is discovering that he is obliged to behave himself – which is why he wants to find another source for gambling funds.'

'Well, with any luck, that might be the last we shall see of him.'

'Do you think so?' asked the earl ironically. 'I suspect that Malcolm will reappear in our lives with monotonous frequency.'

Chapter Sixteen

Once Flora was on the road to recovery, she received many visitors. Jane often came to sit and do her sewing in her room, which was pleasant and soothing, because Jane was quite undemanding company, talking gently of household concerns, local interests, and Roberto's family history, without expecting Flora to make any kind of response. Roberto had looked in with a book full of pictures to look at, and she was ashamed to admit that that was about as much as she could cope with.

Mrs Wylde also came to visit, but her time was chiefly taken up with Catherine, so they generally came together, Catherine often bringing sketches that she had done.

'I do hope that you will soon be well enough to come too, Miss Chayter,' she said. 'I like it when we go sketching together.' To this Flora made no reply.

Matthew, too, came to see her and stayed for a short time, having brought a posy of flowers for her. She thanked him and, as he handed them to Cosette to be arranged, she saw how their fingers touched and lingered. She was delighted to hear of their engagement, but mingled with that delight was a little heartache, because she could not imagine that such happiness would ever be hers. Quite unintentionally, Matthew managed to rub salt into the wound. When Cosette had gone out briefly to find a vase for the flowers, Flora asked him – partly, she had to admit, from a longing just to hear his name – whether the earl had been informed of their attachment. Matthew laughed.

'Yes, and what do you think? He gave us his blessing!'

'Matthew, I'm delighted for you,' she said warmly. Then she added cautiously, 'I have to say that I expected you to have some difficulty convincing him.'

'So did I, but he was as smooth as you please as soon as he realized that. . . .' Colouring up, he stopped speaking and looked at her guiltily.

'Go on,' said Flora quietly.

'It doesn't matter,' said Matthew, and began to speak of other topics. Flora could guess the rest: Craythorne had obviously been so pleased that Matthew was not attached to someone as immoral as herself that he had approved the engagement.

She knew by now that she had nearly drowned, and that Craythorne had rescued her from the water. She had no memory of her illness, however, so she had no idea that it was also Craythorne who had nursed her. As far as she was concerned, nothing had happened to change the contempt in which he held her. She thought sadly that it probably said much for his humanity that he had been prepared to risk his life to save one whom he despised so thoroughly. Of all the people in the household, he was the one who had not been near her. That surely told its own story.

It was not that he had not been tempted. On more than one occasion, he had hesitated outside her door, in a way that was very unlike his normally decisive manner, but each time he had walked away without entering. On one of those occasions, he had encountered Jane walking down the corridor in order to sit with her friend. Jane had been impressed with the tender way in which the earl had cared for Flora and had drawn her own conclusions, both about his concern, and about his previous unreasonable behaviour.

'Why do you not go in?' she asked him.

'Has she asked for me?' he enquired. Jane looked away.

'No,' she answered. 'But I think, perhaps, that you have things to say to her?'

'You are right, of course,' he admitted ruefully. 'But I must confess that I am a little afraid of what she might say in reply. And besides, when I speak to her I want her to be strong enough to stand on her feet and tell me, if she so wishes, that she despises me. I owe her that.'

At last, there came a morning when Flora awoke feeling hungry for the first time. She sat up with Cosette's help and did more justice to her breakfast than she had done since before her illness. The doctor happened to call that day and was delighted with her recovery and clearly inclined to attribute it to his own skill.

'Tomorrow,' he said, 'you may go out.'

'Go out,' murmured Flora, surprised at how excited she felt about the thought.

'Certainly,' replied the doctor, turning to Jane who had come in with him, 'providing she has a very reliable escort.'

'That can be arranged,' said Jane.

Accordingly, the following day Cosette helped Flora to dress for the first time in over a week. Flora was amazed at how loose her clothes felt, how weak she seemed to be and how easily she tired. Fortunately, Cosette was very capable and business-like. She and Matthew were to go with her on her outing. Flora had intended to walk downstairs, but when she stood up for the first time, her legs wobbled so much that it was quite clear that she would have to be carried down. She assumed that it would be Matthew who would have this task, so she was surprised and not a little disconcerted when the door of her chamber opened to reveal Lord Craythorne. He, too, looked as if he had lost a little weight. He looked serious but not at all angry or disapproving. Indeed, had it been possible, Flora might almost have thought that he looked a little diffident. She found herself blushing and one hand went to her throat. To the earl's eyes, with that faint tinge colouring her pale cheeks, she looked adorable.

He enquired gravely after her health, and she found herself murmuring she knew not what in reply. She had not forgotten the bitter exchanges that had taken place between them in the past. She was unsure what his opinion might be of her now, and she did not know how to react to him. She could not pretend that all his bitter words had never been said, but neither could she deny the fact that her heart had leaped at the very sight of him. Despite all that had happened, she loved him still, and she was afraid that in her weakness she would find it harder to conceal her feelings from him. She wondered why he was there, but she was soon to find out, for upon discovering that she was ready for her outing, he bent and picked her up in his arms.

In her delirium, sometime between sleeping and waking, she thought that she had dreamed at times of being held by him, her innermost desires refusing to be crushed by the hopeless situation that existed between them. Now, so close to him that she could feel the beating of his heart, she found herself unable to move, her hands clasped tightly together. He walked with her out of her chamber and down the corridor and, as they reached the top of the stairs, he slackened his grip as if to drop her. She uttered a tiny gasp, and at once her arms went up to wrap themselves around his neck, so that she could save herself. He smiled down at her – the first smile that he had directed at her for a long time now – and said, 'That's better. Now I can keep you safe.' His words were kindly and his tone gentle, and her heart, chilled by his previous cruelty, began to warm. Once downstairs, he carried her past a smiling Jane to the entrance where there was waiting for them not a gondola, but a larger boat with oars and sails.

'Take great care of her,' said Jane. 'She is very precious.'

'Yes, I know,' replied the earl. It was the first time that Flora had come close to the water since her accident and for a moment she trembled a little, one hand clutching at the earl's coat. 'It's all right,' he said, sensitive to her fears. 'I won't let go of you.'

He carried her on board the boat and sat her down on a seat in the bows, making sure that she was comfortable, with adequate shade. She thanked him, warily, then said, 'Where are we going?'

'To Torcello,' he answered. 'I thought that it would be peaceful and not too crowded for your first outing.'

Torcello was the furthest away of all the islands in the lagoon, and after a while, Flora relaxed with the gentle movement of the boat through the water. She could not help comparing this trip with the last water journey in which she had travelled with Lord Craythorne. His thoughtfulness in his choice of destination, his remaining at her side, and his willingness to point out things of interest to her were markedly in contrast to his cold demeanour and contemptuous disregard for her comfort on their way down the Brenta from Padua to Venice.

Cosette remained out of sight, but Matthew joined them from time to time and stood talking quietly with his cousin. They both seemed to understand that Flora did not want too much conversation as yet. Now that she knew them both better, she could not understand how she had ever mistaken one for the other, even momentarily. Matthew's hair was not as dark as his cousin's, nor as wavy, and it was always tied back immaculately, whereas more often than not, Craythorne left his hair to wave loose in the breeze, as it did now. Both men stood there confidently, but Craythorne almost seemed to claim the deck as his own and, even in repose, there was an arrogant tilt to his chin that his cousin lacked.

For his part, Craythorne was pleased with how the outing had gone so far. True, Flora had seemed startled to see him at first, and had been very wary about his carrying her downstairs. But she had not appeared to take offence at the ruse which he had employed in order to persuade her to put her arms around his neck. The feel of her nearness, and her hands touching his nape had almost been his undoing, but he had resolved to take things very slowly. Before any closer relationship could become possible, he must obtain her forgiveness, and persuade her to look upon him as a friend again; something which she had been doing until Milan, when he, like a fool, threw it all away. Now, there were many bridges to build; he must be cautious if he was to avoid wrecking everything.

When they docked at Torcello, Craythorne turned to Flora with a smile.

'By your leave, ma'am,' he said politely, as he made ready to pick her up. As he did so, she experienced a fleeting fragment of memory, and wrinkled her brow in her efforts to pursue it. The earl halted at once. 'Have I hurt you?' he asked her, seeing her frown.

'No, not at all,' she replied. When they reached dry land, she said, 'I would like to try and walk if I may, My Lord.' Carefully he put her down. She found herself to be not quite as unsteady as she had been first thing that morning, but she still felt rather weak and she was glad to have the support of his arm. Under her hand, she felt the strength of his muscles beneath the fine cloth of his coat, and while that reassured her, there was also something about the feel of him that made her heart beat a little faster.

Matthew and Cosette walked behind them for a little while, followed by the servants carrying a hamper, but soon the earl and Flora found themselves taking another route. As they walked, Craythorne explained to her that at one time Torcello had bid fair to rival Venice in size and importance.

'Now look around you,' he said. 'Nothing but ruins! It just goes to show how the plans that men make can come to nothing, doesn't it?'

They visited the Byzantine style Duomo di Sant Maria dell'Assunta and admired the mosaics covering the floor as well as the walls. For Flora it was a wonderful time, and she almost felt as if they were back in the Ambrosian library in Milan, before all the dreadful business with Malcolm had blown up again.

'You are tired,' said the earl eventually, looking at her face. 'Come, let us find somewhere to sit down, and I will go in search of our picnic.' He found a spot amongst the ruins, beneath an old tree where they were able to rest, and made as if to take off his coat for her to sit on.

'No, it's quite all right,' said Flora. 'Look, I really do not need this shawl which Jane pressed upon me. I will sit on that.' She began to remove it from her shoulders, but found that it was caught on the fastening at the back of her gown.

'Allow me,' said the earl, going behind her, and disentangling her shawl with fingers that suddenly seemed to have become all thumbs. Flora closed her eyes and took a deep breath in order to combat the agitation that she felt at his closeness. After they had sat down, Craythorne spoke again. 'Do you want me to seek out our refreshment, or shall we talk first?'

Remembering past conversations, Flora paled a little, but she said bravely, 'If you have something to say to me, My Lord, I would prefer that you said it straight away.' He coloured a little and looked away from her.

'Ah, God, I knew that my past behaviour towards you would come back to haunt me. Flora – Miss Chayter – I have said many things to you that I should never have said. I have treated you in a way that no man who calls himself a gentleman should treat a gently bred woman. I have allowed my imagination to run away with me and as a consequence I have hurt you dreadfully. I do not deserve that you should pardon me, but I am bold enough to ask for your forgiveness all the same.' She made as if to speak, but he held up his hand. 'Pray do not feel that you must answer me straight away,' he said. 'The hurts I have inflicted upon you are severe indeed. God forbid that you should address me as hastily as I have you on occasions.' He paused for a moment. She said nothing, her head bent so that he could not read her expression; and his heart sank. Tentatively, he went on, 'If you feel that you need time before you can consider forgiving me, then I will understand.'

They sat in silence for what seemed to Craythorne to be an eternity. For Flora, this was what she had been longing to hear from him – an admission that he had been mistaken in her. But there was one thing missing, and because she felt that she had already ranked so low in his esteem that she had nothing to lose, she made so bold as to ask for it.

'My Lord, I will not pretend that you have not hurt me, for that would be to tell you a lie. But I know that you treated me as you did because you believed my behaviour to be an affront to your honour. I made one foolish mistake, and on the basis of that you have made sweeping judgements about me. Consequently, it is not your honour that has been affronted but mine. I believe that I would be able to forgive you, if you in your turn would now say from your heart that you believe me to be honourable and . . . and virtuous.'

She looked straight at him then. His colour had risen a little, but he looked back at her and said without hesitation, 'Miss Chayter, I admit to you that I am the one who has acted dishonourably in all this. I believe you to be an honourable and virtuous woman.' There was a brief silence, then he added tentatively, 'Am I forgiven?' She nodded and, gently, he took her hand and raised it to his lips. 'Thank you,' he said, and released it. She put her hand back in her lap. He would never know how much she wanted to raise it to her cheek. She would never know how much he had wanted to turn it over and caress the palm with his lips.

'I feel I must also apologize to you for the behaviour of my sister's cousin,' said the earl a little later. 'I understand that he tried to obtain money from you.'

'No, not from me,' answered Flora. 'He wanted me to beg you for money on his behalf, but I refused. I had come to understand by then that he had already imposed upon you considerably.'

'I'm afraid I am not the only person upon whom he has imposed,' he replied, and Flora blushed bright red. He hurried on, 'However, his days of imposing upon others may be over, I believe. He is now married to a young woman with three formidable brothers, all of whom will make it their business to see that he keeps on the straight and narrow.'

'Perhaps he will now become a reformed character,' murmured Flora.

'One would like to think so,' replied Craythorne. 'He would certainly be an ungrateful dog not to appreciate what a gem he has in his new bride. Besides, he has always had enough charm and address to get himself out of any situation. It would not surprise me if, before long, he has not only managed to bamboozle his new family into signing a huge sum of money over to him, but also to convince them that it was their idea from the very beginning.' The words were ordinary enough, even a little humorous, but there was a definite edge of bitterness to his tone. Flora looked at him questioningly.

'My Lord . . .' she began. He shook his head as if to brush off the mood of reverie.

'Leigh . . . please call me Leigh.' He sighed, and looked at her ruefully. 'Heaven forbid that I should ever envy Malcolm,' he said. 'Although there have been times when I have done so.' He was silent for a moment then went on, 'Shortly after I attained the earldom, about eight years ago, I became engaged to a young lady with whose name I will not burden you. We were attending an outdoor celebration of some kind at my principal residence. Malcolm, just down from Eton, was there. I'd lost sight of my betrothed and I went to look for her. I heard her before she saw me, and she was talking with a friend of hers about me.' He smiled wryly. 'They say eavesdroppers never hear any good of themselves, don't they? My betrothed had seen Malcolm, you see, and was bemoaning the fact that I looked nothing like him. He was far more her idea of what an earl should be like; tall and handsome, whilst I was short and ugly. Then when she saw me, she laughed, and asked me whether I thought she would ever have looked at me had I not been titled and rich.'

'What did you do?' asked Flora, horrified at the story that she was hearing, and filled with a longing to give a certain 'lady' a piece of her mind.

'Do? I'm afraid that I did not act like a gentleman. I ended the engagement. My former betrothed soon found someone as rich as myself, and twice my age, so she was happy. You see, that is how I earned my reputation of being a hard man to cross. Hard and ugly, whereas Malcolm is eternally good-natured, handsome, and of course, dreadfully ill-used.' He sounded so despondent that Flora forgot about caution and modesty in her determination to cheer him up.

'But you aren't ugly,' she protested. 'True, you have a different style of beauty to that of Malcolm.' Craythorne burst into derisive laughter.

'It's the first time that I've ever heard ugliness described as a different style of beauty,' he replied in tones of self-mockery.

'You aren't ugly,' insisted Flora, laying a hand on his arm in her determination to carry her point. 'Your eyes are compelling and your hair is magnificent! And besides, no one as . . . as vital and as masculine as yourself could possibly be described as ugly!' Suddenly, she realized what she had said and how it might be interpreted. Quickly, she moved her hand, and put it back in her lap. Craythorne, looking at her down-bent head, her flushed face and her tightly clasped hands, felt his heart give a leap of hope.

'You are very kind,' he said. Then, greatly daring, he began, 'Miss Chayter . . . Flora. . . .'

'So there you are!' exclaimed Matthew as he and Cosette drew near, followed by the servants with the hamper. 'We were wondering if we were going to have to wait all day for our luncheon, weren't we, Cosette?'

'As *m'sieur* says,' said Cosette demurely, as she began to supervise the disposal of the picnic, and Flora noticed that she gave Matthew a sideways glance that seemed to indicate that the newly engaged couple had not been concerned about food at all. Craythorne stood at their approach, and nobly suppressed the urge to tell his cousin to take Cosette, the picnic and the servants to the other end of the island.

'We've been here for some time,' he said. 'You must have been looking in all the wrong places.' (Or perhaps not looking at all, Flora thought privately to herself.)

When the repast was ready, Cosette sat down next to Matthew in the most unaffected, natural way, which seemed to indicate that she would take her place at Matthew's side without the slightest difficulty. The chicken that had been packed for them was delicious and Flora was surprised to discover how much her appetite had returned just from this little outing in the fresh air.

'That's better,' said Matthew, as he poured them all some more wine. 'You both look as if you have more colour, now that you've escaped from the sickroom!'

Flora looked at Lord Craythorne, her expression puzzled. 'The sickroom? Have you also been ill, My Lord . . . Leigh?'

'No, not at all,' he replied, his brows drawing together in

that familiar bar of disapproval. Flora looked away wondering whether he now regretted asking her to use his Christian name. She did not see that his frown was directed at Matthew, and not at her.

After they had finished their meal, Cosette tidied away the things and the earl gently suggested that Flora might like a stroll.

'Not too far,' he said. 'But I can always carry you if you feel fatigued.' By now, the servants were carrying the basket back to the boat, and Cosette and Matthew had followed, supposedly to supervise. Craythorne helped her to her feet, but when she was almost standing upright, she stepped by accident on the edge of her gown, and stumbled. Quickly the earl caught her in his arms, and in the confusion, she put her hand up and it brushed against his cheek. Suddenly, with his face so close to hers, a vague memory became clear.

'You nursed me!' she exclaimed. 'When I was ill, you nursed me! But why did no one tell me of this?'

'I wouldn't let them tell you,' he answered, gently releasing her. 'I didn't want you to know.' He could see that a denial would be unconvincing and useless.

'Why not?' she asked him. 'Why should I not know of your kindness and tender care, if only to thank you?'

'But that's just it,' he answered, taking hold of her hands. 'I don't want you to feel you owe me anything.'

'Why did you do it, then?' she whispered, looking up into his face.

'I did it because if anything had happened to you, I don't think that I would have wanted to go on living. Flora, I cannot be silent, even if you are shocked by what I have to say. Maybe it's too soon for me to speak, but I have to tell you that I love you. I know that I've been every kind of fool; always seeming to believe the worst of you. Over the last few weeks, I've given you every reason to hate me. The truth is that I have been out of my mind with jealousy of any man who received your smiles or enjoyed your conversation, and all the time I was conducting myself towards you in such a way that no sane woman would want to smile at me or talk to me ever again.

'You say you want to thank me for what I did for you. Well, perhaps I'm being greedy; perhaps I'm longing for the moon; but I don't want your gratitude, I want your love.' Hardly able to believe what she was hearing, she looked at him, her eyes shining.

'It is yours, My Lord,' she replied. He looked at her as if he did not understand that she was telling him the very thing that he wanted to hear. 'Leigh, I love you,' she said, forgetting any embarrassment in her urgent need to make it plain to him. This time he understood her, and she had hardly finished speaking before he gathered her into his arms with great tenderness, and his mouth covered hers. He had kissed her before, but with cruelty; now his embrace was gentle – for he was mindful of her weakened condition – and full of reverence, but with a hint of passion to come.

Much later, the earl said, 'I was convinced that you would want nothing more to do with me. The things I said and did must, I was sure, have wrecked my chances. All I was hoping for today was that you would forgive me, and perhaps allow me to be your friend once more. After that, I was intending to woo you and win you – however long it took.'

'For my part, I was certain that you were enamoured of the countess,' admitted Flora. 'I could not imagine that you could possibly want me when you could have her.'

'My dearest love, you are being very foolish,' replied the earl, the ardent look in his eyes taking away any sting from his words. 'Marianne was a part of my life some years ago, and I renewed my acquaintance with her with some pleasure, but by that time, all my heart was yours, even if I was too stupid to realize it.'

'I never stopped loving you,' confessed Flora, an admission that so moved the earl that he had to kiss her yet again. 'I tried to, after Padua, and then that night in the *palazzo*. . . .'

'Don't remind me,' groaned Craythorne.

'But the trouble was that even whilst I was seething with indignation at what you had said, there was something in me that tempted me quite dreadfully to accept your disgraceful suggestion, in a way that I was never tempted by Malcolm.' They were strolling gently back towards the boat, but now Craythorne stopped and took hold of her hands again, his face suddenly serious.

'You do well to remind me,' he said. 'Flora, on two occasions now I have made you a proposal that dishonoured us both. Today, I want to rectify that. My dear, forgiving angel, will you marry me?'

'Of course I will,' she answered with a barely suppressed gurgle of laughter.

'Now what is it?' he asked, kissing her smiling lips. 'You're not making mockery of me I trust, because if so, ma'am,' he continued, pulling her closer, and punctuating every few words with a kiss, 'I shall have to take stern measures!'

'Certainly not,' replied Flora, as soon as she was able. 'It was when you called me an angel that I had to laugh. You see, that night when you found me with Malcolm and made us come inside, I thought then that you looked like a dark, avenging angel.'

'My word!' he exclaimed, much struck.

'So you see, you cannot be ugly,' went on Flora. 'For whoever heard of an ugly angel?' Craythorne showed his appreciation of her compliment in a most ardent style, and this time his kiss held more than a hint of passion, to which Flora responded with fervour.

'Talking of Malcolm,' he said eventually, 'do you recall that I told you I had been jealous of him?' Flora nodded. 'Then let me tell you another reason why. You see, some months ago, in fact nearly a year ago, my sister took a new governess into her employ. As Catherine's welfare is of great concern to me, I decided to investigate this new employee, to discover whether she was more satisfactory than the string of failures that had preceded her. I met this new governess, and was at once enchanted. The little conversation I had with her encouraged me to think that she was as intelligent as she was lovely. I came away resolved to see her again, but I wanted to be cautious. I was not looking for a dishonourable liaison, and I did not want to do anything to compromise her or damage her reputation.

'Then a matter of business here in Venice came to my attention and I had to make arrangements for foreign travel. Letty also asked for my escort to visit Jane, so I was doubly bound to go. However, I was quite determined to see this lovely young woman again. I was hoping that perhaps through Catherine, I might begin a correspondence with her that might lead to other things. So I hurried down from London to my sister's house intending to spend the maximum time possible there, only to discover that Malcolm had beaten me once again.'

'Leigh! Oh no!' exclaimed Flora, secretly pleased at his admission, and rather proud of herself that she was managing to call him by his name.

'I'm afraid so. So now you see why I was so angry: the woman I had hoped to make my own had already shown a preference for Malcolm.'

'Not for long,' she assured him, 'I was lonely when I met Malcolm, but I soon realized that you are worth a thousand Malcolms!' He smiled down at her, and drew her close to him, and they kissed once again. For both of them, loneliness was over; they had each other.

Bibliography

Booker, John, *Travellers' Money*, (Sutton Publishing Ltd, 1994)

Hibbert, Christopher, *The Grand Tour*, (Methuen, 1987)

Lowe, Alfonso, *La Serenessima – The Last Flowering of the Venetian Republic*, (Cassell, 1974)

Piozzi, Hester Lynch, *Observations and Reflections made in the Course of a Journey Through France, Italy and Germany*, ed. Herbert Barrows, (University of Michigan Press, USA, 1967)

Toynbee, ed., *Letters of Horace Walpole*, (Oxford Clarendon Press, 1903)

Vaussard, Maurice, *Daily Life in Eighteenth Century Italy* (George Allen & Unwin Ltd, 1962)